D0112311

Books by Mark Cheverton

The Gameknight999 Series
Invasion of the Overworld
Battle for the Nether
Confronting the Dragon

The Mystery of Herobrine Series: A Gameknight999 Adventure
Trouble in Zombie-town
The Jungle Temple Oracle
Last Stand on the Ocean Shore

Herobrine Reborn Series: A Gameknight999 Adventure
Saving Crafter
Destruction of the Overworld
Gameknight999 vs. Herobrine

Herobrine's Revenge Series: A Gameknight999 Adventure
The Phantom Virus
Overworld in Flames
System Overload

The Birth of Herobrine: A Gameknight999 Adventure
The Great Zombie Invasion
Attack of the Shadow-Crafters
Herobrine's War

The Mystery of Entity303: A Gameknight999 Adventure
Terrors of the Forest
Monsters in the Mist
Mission to the Moon

The Gameknight999 Box Set
The Gameknight999 vs. Herobrine Box Set
The Gameknight999 Adventures Through Time Box Set

The Rise of the Warlords: A Far Lands Adventure
Zombies Attack!
Bones of Doom
Into the Spiders' Lair

Wither War: A Far Lands Adventure
The Wither King
The Withers Awaken
The Wither Invasion (Coming Soon!)

THE WITHERS AWAKEN

WITHER WAR BOOK TWO: **A FAR LANDS ADVENTURE**

AN UNOFFICIAL MINECRAFTER'S ADVENTURE

MARK CHEVERTON

SKY PONY PRESS
NEW YORK

Copyright © 2018 by Mark Cheverton

Minecraft® is a registered trademark of Notch Development AB

The Minecraft game is copyright © Mojang AB

Sky Pony Press books may be purchased in bulk at special discounts for sales promotion, corporate gifts, fund-raising, or educational purposes. Special editions can also be created to specifications. For details, contact the Special Sales Department, Sky Pony Press, 307 West 36th Street, 11th Floor, New York, NY 10018 or info@skyhorsepublishing.com.

Sky Pony® is a registered trademark of Skyhorse Publishing, Inc.®, a Delaware corporation.

Visit our website at www.skyponypress.com.

10 9 8 7 6 5 4 3 2 1

Library of Congress Cataloging-in-Publication Data is available on file.

Cover design by Brian Peterson
Cover artwork by Vilandas Sukutis (www.veloscraft.com)
Technical consultant: Gameknight999

Print ISBN: 978-1-51073-489-0
Ebook ISBN: 978-1-51073-492-0

Printed in the United States of America

ACKNOWLEDGMENTS

As always, I want to thank my family for all their support while I was writing this book. Their continual faith in me is an inspiration that keeps me writing page after page.

NOTE FROM THE AUTHOR

I had a fantastic time writing this book, as well as the last—I think this has been my favorite of all the series I've written. I'm really enjoying writing about Krael and his wither army, and based on feedback I've received about the first book in this series, all of you are enjoying it as well. I can't wait to start the third book in this series, *Wither Invasion.* Writing about withers, for some reason, is incredibly exciting. Maybe because every time I try to battle one of them, I'm always killed. This is my revenge.

I've given you a lot of lore to play with in these *Wither War* books, so I'm looking forward to seeing the stories the young writers out there create. I hope some of you write about the Great War between the NPC wizards and monster warlocks. Maybe some of you will write about how the withers were created, or what role they played in the Great War.

For those who want to write and are just afraid to try, I have numerous writing tutorials on my website, www.markcheverton.com. Just click on the *Writing Tutorials* tab or on the *Writing Tips from Mark* tab and you can see all of my writing videos. Hopefully, these will help you with your own writing.

Please send me your stories; I post every story I receive on my website. Click on the FanFic/Art tab and you can see the hundreds of stories I've posted over the years. You can email me your story through my website, www.markcheverton.com, but be sure you type your email address correctly, so I can send you a link once I've posted it.

If you have questions for me, send me an email. If you want to hear about how fat my cat is, send me an email. If you want to know anything, or have a comment, or want to tell me which is your favorite book, send me an email. I reply to every email, as long as you type your email address correctly. I can't wait to hear from you all!

Keep reading, and watch out for creepers.

Mark Cheverton (Monkeypants_271)

People matter, and stuff doesn't. If someone judges you based on your hair or your clothes or your phone or anything else like that, then they don't know you well enough to look past all the stuff and see the inner light burning bright within you. Cling to the inner light that makes you unique, harness it and let it grow. . . . Everything else is just noise.

CHAPTER 1

The darkness wrapping around Krael, the king of the withers, was like a leaden blanket of hopelessness. He had tried to free the many withers floating high overhead—his wither army—but that annoying boy-wizard had thwarted his efforts.

"I'll make that wizard suffer somehow," the center head hissed vengefully, the right and left skulls nodding.

Krael glanced upward, his eyes instantly drawn to his wife, Kora, floating in the center of the huge cavern. The redstone lanterns distributed across the Cave of Slumber cast a soft yellow glow, illuminating her body. Kora's three heads lolled to the side, eyes shut as she continued the three-hundred-year-long nap caused by the magical spells built into the Cave of Slumber. Those enchantments had ensnared Kora and the hundreds of other withers here during the Great War between the NPC wizards and monster warlocks, drawing them into a perpetual sleep.

And now, those spells were trying to capture the king of the withers as well.

Krael lay on his side on the bottom of the gigantic chamber, too weak to fly, but still awake. The enchantments in the two magical Crowns of Skulls on his left and center heads cast an iridescent purple glow upon his surroundings. The magical Crowns fought against the spells woven into the Cave, allowing him to resist falling into an eternal sleep . . . for now.

"We must move, or we'll die here." Krael's voice was weak but insistent.

The wither king lifted his body off the ground and stood on the end of his stubby spine. He had no legs, and usually didn't need them, for withers could fly, but right now, he didn't have the strength to float up into the air.

"I see something glowing," the right skull said.

Even though the wither was exhausted, Right's voice still had a lyrical and soothing sound, as usual. "We must move that way and see what it is."

"What's the point?" Left's scratchy voice sounded hopeless.

"Because it might be something to help us." Right's voice now had an angry edge.

Krael inched slowly across the ground, his dark spine dragging across the stone floor, a scraping sound echoing off the cold stone walls. As they neared the source of the glow, Krael's breathing quickened, his pounding heartbeat like a drum; the light ahead was an iridescent purple, like that of an enchanted artifact. It could be some weapon, dropped there by the ancient wizards as they were building the Cave, or maybe some enchanted tool used to create the insidious spells trapping the withers in an eternal prison, or maybe it could be . . . Krael didn't even want to consider that.

"I saw the boy-wizard drop it," Right said.

"Yeah," Left added. "He dropped it when our flaming skull struck him. The fool can't hold on to anything."

"Be quiet," Center snapped. "Just focus on getting to whatever it is. We'll know when we reach it."

"If . . . we reach it," Left yawned. "I'm getting sleepier and sleepier."

Krael slid forward, trying to move faster, though his

stubby spine was getting sore as it dragged across the rough, stone floor. The glow was becoming brighter, the distant artifact pulsing with power as he neared. At the same time, the two Crowns of Skulls atop his head also started to pulse, their glittering purple glow in sync with the object up ahead.

Right could barely keep her eyes open now. Without a Crown of Skulls on her head, the enchantments from the Cave of Slumber felt stronger; their whispers and promises of blissful sleep echoed in Right's mind, drawing her eyelids down, and down, and . . . a loud snore filled the air as her head flopped to the side, asleep.

"We must hurry," Center hissed desperately. Left, also struggling with fatigue, just grunted.

Krael moved across the uneven floor, the scraping sound of his spine across the hard floor now mixing with the wheezing snores from Right. He could see it now. The item ahead was gold and shiny, its magical enchantments lighting the cave floor with a sparkling glow. He was getting close . . .

"I can see it, Left. I can see it. It's the third Crown of Skulls! If we can reach it, the third Crown will give us enough power to resist the Cave of Slumber and get out of here." Center's voice was filled with excitement at first, but then grew concerned. "Left . . . are you okay?"

Another snore pierced the dark cave; Left had fallen asleep as well, his skull drooping forward.

"I don't have much time." Center could feel his own eyelids growing heavier and heavier.

Using every ounce of his remaining strength, Krael made one giant leap forward. His protruding spine left the ground and floated through the air just for an instant. For a moment, he thought he was going to make it, but then his spine touched the ground again, slowing his body to a grinding halt, still too far away to reach the Crown.

"No . . . NO!" Rage filled Krael as he stared at his prize, just out of reach.

Leaning forward, the wither king extended his body, trying once more to reach the Crown, but he was so tired. Maybe just a quick nap and he'd then have the energy to get the Crown. Slowly, he closed his eyes, but he was leaning too far over now, and lost his balance. His body fell forward and landed on the discarded Crown of Skulls. Instantly, the ancient artifact zipped into his inventory, adding to the magical enchantments woven through his body. A surge of power blasted through Krael, immediately snapping all three skulls awake, their eyes wide with surprise as the new Crown suddenly appeared atop Right's head.

With the complete set of Crowns, power on a scale never before seen in Minecraft surged through the wither king's body. Sparks of purple lightning wrapped around his body as waves of iridescent energy moved across his body as if they were living things.

"YES!" Center exclaimed, a huge smile on his face. He glanced at Left and Right, then floated up into the air. Rising through the darkness, he moved closer to his wife, staring at her sleeping form. "I'll have you out of here soon, Kora."

Krael floated even higher, then faced one of the cavern walls.

"There, fire your flaming skulls," Center commanded. "But first, let the power from the Crowns fill you."

The other skulls nodded, then concentrated. The three Crowns of Skulls grew bright as sparks jumped from one to the next, crawling across the back of Krael's heads like tiny, shimmering spiders. And then the wither king fired.

A barrage of flaming skulls streaked through the air and smashed into the cavern's wall. Sandstone cubes, enveloped by the fiery grasp of the explosion, disintegrated from sight, releasing blocks of sand which fell to the cavern floor. But the wall still stood, its surface shining bright with magical enchantments, the spells making the Cave wall indestructible.

"You aren't indestructible anymore," Krael smiled at the wall, then glanced at the other two skulls. "Fire again."

They gathered their magic, letting the power envelop their flaming skulls . . . then fired. Nine flaming skulls smashed into the glittering wall with the strength of a giant's fist. The Cave of Slumber shook, causing more blocks of sand to fall from the walls and ceiling, but the wall still stood without a scratch or dent.

Krael moved closer, his anger rising. "Gather more magical power."

The wither used the enchantments in the Crowns of Skulls, drawing as much energy as they could from the ancient artifact and allowing it to build within the monster's three dark skulls. The dark skin of the wither king soon gave off a faint purple glow which grew brighter and brighter as the Crowns grew dimmer.

"NOW!"

The three heads fired their skulls at the sparkling cavern wall. Blazing bright as the sun, the flaming skulls smashed into the sandstone barrier, blasting through the wall and carving a massive hole in the side of the Cave of Slumber. For the first time in over three hundred years, the early morning sunlight streamed into the cavern.

Krael smiled, then turned and floated back to his wife, Kora. Moving behind her, he pushed her toward the newly made exit. When the sleeping wither moved out of the Cave, her heads slowly rose and her eyes blinked open, full of uncertainty.

"What's happening . . . I'm getting sleepy . . . we're trapped!" She sounded terrified.

"It's alright, wife. I've saved you." Krael moved closer to Kora and leaned his center skull forward against hers.

"Krael . . . you didn't get trapped in that cave?" She glanced up at the three crowns on her husband's head and gasped in surprise. "You have the Crowns?"

The wither king nodded. "Yes, and I just used them to rescue you, but now we need to free the others, and the spells in the Cave will try to ensnare you again. Fly fast and follow me."

Krael streaked into the Cave of Slumber and moved behind the nearest wither as his wife moved to another. They pushed the two withers out of the Cave, then explained the situation once they awoke. Then, the four of them entered the cavern and rescued four more, then eight, then sixteen, then . . .

In twenty minutes, they'd rescued hundreds of monsters from the Cave, the withers all snarling with confusion and rage.

Krael floated high into the air and stared down at his new army. "Brothers and sisters, you have slept a long time. More than three centuries have passed." The withers glanced at each other, shocked, as the wither king continued.

"The wizards who imprisoned you are all gone. The monster warlocks were defeated. Again, the NPCs rule the surface of Minecraft and care nothing for the rights of monsters. Skeletons, zombies, endermen, spiders—all the monsters must hide in shadowy caves and tunnels, fearing for their lives if discovered by villagers." The withers grumbled as angry words spread throughout the army.

Krael glanced down at his wife. Kora gave him a smile that filled him with a moment of joy, but then the image of the young wizard, Watcher, floated into his mind, and his three skulls frowned.

"But we still have an enemy." Amplified by the three Crowns of Skulls, Krael's voice boomed across the desert landscape. "A boy-wizard tried to stop me from rescuing you. He is likely still in this world. We're going to destroy this puny wizard, then go back to the Far Lands and begin our revenge. With the three Crowns of Skulls and all of you at my back, nothing can stop us."

The withers cheered, some firing their flaming skulls into the air.

"We will not stop until the boy-wizard is destroyed. Then, we will take our revenge on the ancient wizards who trapped you in the Cave of Slumber by exterminating every NPC in the Far Lands." Krael laughed cruelly. "Soon, all of Minecraft will belong to the withers!"

The shadowy monsters cheered as Krael stared down at his wife, Kora. She smiled, then fired her own flaming skulls into the sky, an expression of violent glee in her eyes.

CHAPTER 2

Watcher moved through the dark passage, the iridescent glow coming from his arms and chest lighting the corridor. The rest of the NPCs followed close behind, all of them nervous about being in the Labyrinth again.

"You know, last time we were in these passages, many of us thought we'd die in here," Blaster said.

Watcher glanced over his shoulder at the boy, but he was nearly invisible; his black leather armor allowed him to blend in with the darkness, though his perpetual smile gave his presence away.

"I know, but last time, we got out of here because of my magical powers." Watcher's voice sounded proud.

"Here we go," Planter said, sounding resigned. "We know you're a wizard and you have all these magical powers. How could we forget? You keep reminding us."

Blaster and Cutter laughed.

"Well, I do have magical powers." Watcher stopped and turned to look at his friends, then pointed at his girlfriend, Planter. "But I see the glow coming from your arms as well. You have the same magic running through you, too—just not as much."

Planter sighed. "I know." She lowered her head to stare at the ground.

"I see something." Mapper moved next to Watcher and stared into the dim tunnel. "I think that's the room up ahead."

Watcher turned and gazed down the tunnel, his sharp eyesight trying to pierce the darkness. "I think you're right, Mapper. Come on, everyone."

Patting the old man on the back, Watcher continued onward through the passage. After going a couple dozen blocks farther, the tunnel ended in a large, circular chamber with walls and floors made of obsidian. It had the same feel as the first time they'd been here, ancient. The air still smelt stale with a thick layer of dust covering most surfaces, the footprints from the last time they'd been here still clearly visible on the floor. It was likely they were the only people to visit this place since the end of the Great War.

"I wonder how the ancient wizards built the Labyrinth?" Mapper moved to one of the many bookcases to look at the books on the shelves. He pulled one from the shelf and it crumbled into dust, coating his chain-mail-covered boots. He glanced at Watcher with a sad expression on his wrinkled old face. "To build this complex set of tunnels under the huge mountains above us . . . umm . . . what were they called again?"

"The Creeper's Teeth," Blaster said.

"You're so smart." Fencer moved to the boy's side, smiling. After he'd saved Fencer from the attack of an ancient zombie warrior, the young girl's infatuation had been focused on him.

Blaster instantly retreated, moving to the opposite side of the room, which made Watcher smile—he'd been the target of Fencer's affections before, and Blaster had thought it funny. Now the tables were turned a bit.

"That's right, the Creeper's Teeth." Mapper nodded. "I wonder if the wizards made the Creeper's Teeth first or the Labyrinth."

"Who cares?" Cutter's voice boomed off the chamber walls. The big NPC stepped closer to the shiny mirror and stared at his reflection. "It would be nice if we had some more light."

"I only have one torch. Does anyone have any spare torches?" Mapper glanced at the faces of their companions.

There were eighteen villagers and one zombie in their company, and they'd used most of their resources getting to the Cave of Slumber and stopping the wither king.

The other NPCs shook their heads.

"Watcher, you could do that magic thing with your little magic wand," Blaster said.

"Sure, I don't mind, as long as someone has a potion of healing ready for me." Watcher reached into his inventory. His fingers brushed against the fragile Elytra wings his sister had given him before they left the Wizards Tower weeks ago. He was glad he'd been able to repair them after the crash in the Cave of Slumber; she'd be mad if he'd broken them.

Reaching in farther, his fingers found what he was searching for, and he pulled out the Wand of Cloning. The magical artifact was a stick with metal wrapped around its ends, and was shaped like a "Y," as if the wand had been split down the center partway, each half identical.

"Is this really necessary?" Planter asked. "I don't like you using magic when it isn't necessary."

"It's no big deal. I have more than enough power to use this wand." Watcher sounded proud of himself.

"Here we go again," Blaster laughed, shaking his head.

Planter rolled her eyes. "You see, that's the problem. You always think you have enough power, and it's true . . . until it isn't true anymore, and then what happens?"

"You don't need to worry, Planter; I'm a wizard, and I know what I'm doing." Watcher motioned for Mapper to give him the torch.

"I remember when you used that wand the last time." Mapper handed the torch to Watcher, then moved to a nearby bookcase. "Won't the torches last for only a short while before they disappear?"

Watcher nodded. "You're right. The things the Wand of Cloning creates are only temporary, but we won't be here long enough for it to matter. Everyone, stand back."

Watcher placed the torch on the ground, then held the split wand in the air. He moved it over his head, then pointed it at the unlit torch and flicked his wrist multiple times. A bright flash of light filled the air, forcing everyone to look away. Watcher grunted as pain exploded through his body as the wand drew on his health for power. Blaster threw a splash potion of healing against his back, the liquid instantly quenched the flames of agony raging through his body. The young wizard breathed a sigh of relief, then put the wand away as beads of sweat tumbled down his forehead.

"You did it." Mapper bent over and picked up the torches, then moved around the room, placing them on the walls and floors.

The flickering light revealed what they had all expected to see: beds grouped against one wall, old and dusty bookcases positioned all throughout the room, multiple passages leading into the chamber, and a single mirror-like structure against the wall.

"Great, now let's get out of here." Cutter moved to the shining mirror, then motioned for Watcher to come near. "Do your wizard thing and open this doorway."

"Maybe we should wait. There is so much we could learn here." Mapper pulled a book from the bookcase. It crumbled into dust, just like the first had. He glanced at Watcher with a sad expression on his wrinkled, old face. "For example, I thought we'd come through the mirror because that was the way we left the Labyrinth last time. It would have made sense we'd return the same way, but instead, we came in through one of those tunnels."

"It's possible the wizards made the Labyrinth so that you always enter through the tunnels and exit through the mirror." Watcher moved to the old man's side and brushed some of the book dust from his shoulders.

Cutter banged impatiently on the silver mirror with a fist, then glanced at Mapper. "I don't care about how any of this works." The big warrior turned to Watcher. "How about you make this thing work again so we can get out of here?"

"I'm too tired after using the wand, but Planter should be able to do it. I have faith in her." Watcher wiped sweat from his brow again. "It'll take me a few minutes before I feel better."

Mapper reached for another book, the ancient tome crumbling apart just like the first two, though this time, it coated him *and* Watcher with dust. "Oops." The old man tried to wipe the dust off Watcher, but his hands were covered in it, and just made it worse.

"Mapper . . ." Watcher complained.

"Sorry, I can't resist myself." The old man smiled at him, abashed.

Planter stepped closer to the mirror, her long blond hair hanging down over her iron armor. In the flickering light from the torches, it looked like a waterfall of gold spilling down her shoulders; it was beautiful.

"How does it work?" she asked.

"I spoke the truth and then placed my palm on the mirror." Watcher sneezed as he inhaled the dust floating in the air.

Planter stepped up next to Cutter and pressed her square palm onto the mirror.

"Now speak the truth," Watcher said.

Taking a deep breath, she spoke. "I hate magic. I hate the harm it causes and the price it demands from those around it. I wish magic had never come into existence in Minecraft."

Watcher was about to ask if that's how she really

felt when the mirror dissolved, revealing a set of stairs leading up to the surface.

Cutter patted her on the back. "Excellent . . . now let's get out of here. This place gives me the creeps."

The huge warrior drew his diamond sword and moved up the stairs, the other villagers following. Blaster sprinted for the opening, hoping to lose Fletcher, but the girl kept up with him step for step. It made Watcher laugh.

"I heard that." Blaster glanced over his shoulder at Watcher, then disappeared up the steps.

Er-Lan moved to Planter's side. The zombie spoke in a low voice, but his words echoed off the obsidian and quartz walls, letting Watcher hear what he said.

"Er-Lan understands how Planter feels."

"You do?" Planter replied.

The zombie nodded. "Er-Lan also dislikes magic. At times, it can demand much of its wielders and those around them. History tells of many NPCs and monsters corrupted by magic. All should be wary of its tempting power."

"I totally agree, Er-Lan." Planter gave the zombie a huge hug, then the two of them headed up the stairs, side-by-side.

"Mapper, you ready?" Watcher asked, frowning after Planter and Er-Lan's talk.

The old man nodded, then followed Watcher up the stairs.

The steps led them to the surface, spilling them into the desert. The sun was barely above the eastern horizon, its morning rays coating the landscape with warmth; after being in the dark, cold tunnels of the Labyrinth, it felt fantastic.

Behind them, a range of mountains soared into the sky. They were the Creeper's Teeth, and they separated the rest of the world from the Cave of Slumber and the sleeping wither army. Horrific shouts and growls echoed from the steep slopes of the mountains, where twisted and distorted monsters scoured the mountain-side, waiting for the unwary to try and climb over the Teeth; it was part of the ancient wizards' strategy to protect their sleeping wither prisoners.

Putting the mountains and the Labyrinth to their backs, the party headed south, each of them happy to get away from all those withers trapped within the Cave of Slumber.

Suddenly, pain enveloped Watcher as if he were aflame. He screamed and fell to the ground, writhing in agony. A moment later, Planter screamed as well, falling at Er-Lan's feet. The zombie instantly knelt and held her in his clawed hands.

"Watcher, Planter . . . what's wrong?" Mapper pulled out a potion of healing and tossed it to Blaster, then pulled out another and held it to Watcher's lips.

The young boy pushed the bottle away. "No . . . it's something else . . . something magic." Then he and Planter both screamed simultaneously, as if their agony was somehow synchronized.

Er-Lan gritted his teeth and grunted, as if also feeling their pain. The zombie leaned over to help Planter, but then fell to the ground, almost unconscious. Blaster pulled out an apple and offered it to the zombie, then held the potion of healing out to Planter.

"No." She shook her head. "Watcher's right, this is something else."

"What do we do? How can we help you?" Blaster asked.

Suddenly, their screams of agony ceased. Watcher lay on the ground for a moment, waiting in fear for the pain to return, but it seemed to have passed. He sat up, momentarily dizzy, waited for his head to clear, then carefully stood. He ran to Planter and helped her to her feet, then glanced down at Er-Lan.

"Are you okay?" Watcher extended a hand and helped the zombie to his feet.

Er-Lan nodded. "Perhaps it was hunger. This zombie

hasn't eaten for a while." He took a bite out of the apple and shuffled away from Watcher.

"Planter, are you okay?" Watcher put an arm around her.

She nodded, then turned to look him in the eyes. "Something bad happened. I could feel it."

"Me too." Watcher nodded.

"It felt like someone stuck a knife into the fabric of Minecraft." She glanced at her companions who were now gathered around the two wizards. "I fear something terrible has happened, and we aren't gonna like it."

"How do we find out what it is?" Mapper asked.

"I know how." Watcher reached into his inventory and pulled out the Flail of Regrets.

He'd found the ancient weapon during one of their adventures. It was made centuries ago, during the Great War between the NPC wizards and monster warlocks, centuries ago. Somehow, there was the mind of someone or something woven into the weapon. Sometimes, the presence spoke to him; Watcher hoped this was one of those times.

"Flail, are you there?" Watcher spoke aloud to let the others hear, but it wasn't necessary; the Flail could also hear his thoughts.

Of course I'm here . . . where else would I be? The Flail's deep voice resonated within Watcher's mind.

He nodded to the others. "What was that we felt? It was as if—"

The withers are free from the Cave of Slumber. There was a cold, almost hopeless sound to the voice.

Watcher's face went pale.

"What is it?" Blaster asked. "By the look on your face, I'd say it isn't good."

"The withers are on the loose." Planter's voice was weak and shook a bit with fear. Because of her magical powers, she could hear the voice as well.

"What?!" Cutter exclaimed. "I thought we trapped the wither king in the Cave of Slumber, and—"

Watcher held up a hand to silence the big warrior, then turned his attention to the magical weapon in his hand.

What happened? Watcher's words trembled in his head, just like Planter's had. He too was afraid of the terrible wither king, Krael.

The wither king somehow blasted through the walls of the Cave of Slumber, the enchanted weapon said. *He freed hundreds of his fellow withers, and I'm sure he's not happy with you and your friends.*

"The Flail said Krael broke through the walls of the Cave of Slumber. He and his army of withers are on the move," Watcher said.

My name isn't 'Flail'; it's Baltheron! The deep voice boomed angrily through Watcher's mind like a blast from a block of TNT.

"Sorry." Watcher rubbed his ears and shook his head; it ached a little. "He said his name is Baltheron."

"Great, a weapon with a name." Blaster laughed. "What's next . . . is he a wizard too?"

"I don't know if he's a wizard or not," Watcher replied.

OF COURSE I'M A WIZARD! Baltheron paused for a moment, then continued. *I was there during the Great War when everything seemed hopeless. I was there when many wizards followed my lead and we sacrificed ourselves by putting our minds and powers into these weapons. I was there when we turned back the tide, defeated the monster warlocks, and imprisoned the withers.* Baltheron paused again, allowing his words to sink in. *Of course I'm a wizard. Actually, I'm the wizard—the most powerful of those who sacrificed themselves.*

"Yep, he's a wizard." Watcher smiled at his friends.

He could feel anger in the back of his head from the enchanted weapon.

"So, Baltheron, what do we do now?" Watcher stared down at the Flail, his face creased with worry.

Standing around here, waiting for the withers to arrive, isn't the best idea. I'm guessing the wither king will want to punish all of you for interfering with his plans. If I were you, I'd get moving . . . fast.

Watcher nodded, then looked up at his friends. "He says we need to move before the withers find us."

"That's good advice, but how do we stop them?" Blaster drew his two curved knives and spun them between his fingers as if the razor-sharp weapons were just toys.

Watcher shook his head. "I don't know, but we can't stay here; we're too exposed."

"If we have to fight, that round structure with the trees would make a good spot." Cutter drew his diamond sword and held it at the ready.

"You mean The Compass?" Mapper asked.

Cutter nodded. "Let's get there as fast as possible. I'm sure Watcher will have some plan ready by the time we get there . . . right?" He glanced at Watcher.

All eyes turned toward the young wizard with the Flail of Regrets glowing bright in his hand.

"Well . . . sure, I'll come up with something," Watcher said, though he didn't include the *I hope* that resonated in his mind.

"Great." Cutter banged his diamond sword against his enchanted iron armor, making the chest plate ring like a gong. "Let's run."

The big NPC turned and sprinted to the south, the other NPCs following him. Watcher stood there, staring at his friends' backs, trying to think up a plan that would allow them to defeat a couple of hundred flying terrors, the withers, with their small company. It seemed impossible, but he had to think of something. With a firm grip on the Flail's handle, he sprinted south, following his friends as fear and uncertainty filled his mind.

CHAPTER 3

An uneasy silence filled the air as the companions ran through the desolate landscape. They'd moved through the desert for about an hour, putting the Creeper's Teeth and the Labyrinth far behind. When the party passed into this new, dismal biome, Watcher and the others gaped at the destruction levied upon the land. At one time, it had been a forest, with thick patches of grass and clusters of shrubs dotting the ground, but now, it was a lifeless, gray wasteland. The tree branches were completely bare, devoid of any leaves. To Watcher, it made the limbs look like forlorn, outstretched arms, with the narrower branches resembling long, menacing fingers reaching into the sky. It was sad . . . and creepy.

As they ran, their footsteps crushed the dry, gray grass underfoot, causing the blades to crumble into powder. It created an ashen cloud on the ground, hiding their feet, but fortunately, most of the dust stayed near the ground; the NPCs didn't have to breathe too much of it into their lungs. The entire landscape was a sad sight, amplifying Watcher's sense of dread.

"I still can't imagine what kind of magic did this level of destruction to the land here." Mapper coughed, then pulled out a flask of water and took a long drink.

"The magic of the wizards and warlocks can have unexpected consequences." Er-Lan's sad eyes scanned the dead forest. "Many stories were told by our zombie history-keepers about terrible accidents during the Great War that took the lives of many monsters."

"I'm sure the wizards weren't upset about that," Cutter said.

Er-Lan glared at the warrior. "Any death is sad, regardless of whether it is monster or villager. Life should be cherished and not made disposable."

"Tell that to the withers." Blaster moved to the zombie's side, running in lockstep. "I'm sure the wither king and his army would be happy to dispose of us." He glanced at Watcher. "It would be good to know what the withers are doing right now. Why don't you use that thing you took from the spider warlord?"

Watcher nodded, then slowed to a walk. "Does anyone have a healing potion? The Eye of Searching demands a high price, and it can only be paid with HP."

"Why would the wizards make these and have them cause such terrible pain?" Mapper asked.

"Maybe they were reminding others that magic is dangerous and should only be used when necessary." Planter glanced at Watcher. "Is this necessary?"

Watcher nodded. "I think so. We need to know what Krael is doing. Besides, what's the point of having all these incredible magical relics if we aren't gonna use them?"

Planter lowered her gaze to the ground, then spoke, her voice barely a whisper. "Magical things are not more valuable than people. The wielder is always more important than the weapon, because the person holding the sword can choose not to use it; the sword has no choice. Are you the wielder or the weapon?"

Uncertainty flooded through Watcher; did she want him to reply? *Sometimes I'm the wielder,* he thought, *but other times, I know I have to be the weapon.* He didn't know how to respond, so he just stayed silent and continued on his task.

Removing his diamond helmet, Watcher handed it to Mapper, then pulled the Eye of Searching from his inventory. The ancient artifact was a magical item Shakaar, the spider warlord, had used to see where Watcher and his friends were and what they were doing. The spider warlord had planned multiple traps with the enchanted tool and caused many villagers to lose their lives, so Watcher was glad to keep it out of any other monsters' hands.

The Eye was a glass lens with two leather straps attached to either side. It glittered with magical power, the morning light making the iridescent glow seem even brighter than usual. The purple light from the device lit Watcher with a lavender glow, the enchantments woven into the Eye pulsing like a heartbeat, then growing quicker as if the magical item could somehow sense Watcher's presence. Tying the straps behind his head, Watcher positioned the lens over an eye, then gritted his teeth. Instantly, the magical device reached into his HP and drained some of his health, using his health to power its enchantments. Watcher grunted as pain exploded in his head. It felt as if he was on fire, though he knew the flames were only in his mind.

Focusing on his enemy, Watcher thought about Krael, the king of the withers. Instantly, an image of the monster formed in his head. The creature was floating through the air with a huge army of withers following close behind. Three Crowns of Skulls sat atop his dark heads, each glowing angrily with magical power.

"So that's how he got out," Watcher mumbled.

Another wave of pain surged through his body. Watcher grunted again and clenched his teeth, accidentally biting his tongue; the taste of warm blood filled his mouth. He focused his attention away from his agony and onto his enemy again, and Krael appeared in his mind, the golden Crowns bright against the monster's dark skin. Watcher moved his mind away from Krael, trying to see the creature's surroundings. Behind the wither king floated a hundred withers, maybe two hundred, each wearing angry expressions on their dark skulls. Below them was a sandy desert, its green, prickly cacti the only feature visible on the pale ground.

With his mind, Watcher moved around the army until he was behind the horde. Before them stood a huge mountain range: the Creeper's Teeth.

"They're still on the other side of the Teeth," Watcher said in a weak voice.

More pain blasted through him. Something crashed into his back . . . a healing potion, its soothing liquid running beneath his armor and sinking into his skin.

Watcher moved his mind to the front of the withers' formation, trying to get a better view of the entire army. Suddenly, Krael stopped flying, causing the entire horde to become motionless in mid-air. All of the creatures glanced around, probably looking for threats, all except one: Krael. The wither king stared straight at Watcher, his six hateful eyes all focused on him.

"They can see me," Watcher whispered, shocked.

"You tried to imprison me in the Cave of Slumber, boy," Krael shouted furiously, his voice booming across the desert, amplified by the Crowns of Skulls. "Like a pathetic fool, you did a poor job of it. Now, with the third Crown of Skulls in my possession, you don't stand a chance against me and my army. We will make every one of your friends suffer while you watch, then destroy you last. Prepare yourself, boy-wizard, for a storm is coming . . . a wither storm."

Then Krael flew straight at Watcher, his eyes filled with a violent rage.

Reaching up quickly, Watcher pulled off the Eye of Searching, his whole body shaking. Falling to one knee, Watcher stuffed the ancient artifact into his inventory and glanced up at his friends.

"Krael has probably two hundred withers with him." Watcher slowly stood and pulled out an apple from his inventory, quickly devouring the fruit. "He wants revenge."

"Against us?" Planter asked.

Watcher lowered his gaze. "No, not us. He wants revenge against *me*. Krael said he was gonna destroy all of you while I watched, then save me for last."

"You really have a knack for making others hate you." Blaster smiled. "Let's see, first it was the zombie warlord, then the skeleton warlord."

"Don't forget the spider warlord," Cutter added.

"Okay . . . okay, so monsters don't like me much." Watcher scowled as Blaster and Cutter chuckled. "What's important is we need to have a plan, and right now, we're just running away."

"Running away isn't such a bad idea," Mapper said.

"That's true," Er-Lan said. "That is, until those chasing finally catch up."

"Exactly." Watcher patted the zombie on the back. "We need a plan."

Everyone grew silent, each glancing at the others, waiting for someone to speak up. After a long pause, Planter stepped forward, put a hand under her chest plate, and drew out the amulet she'd found before they chased after the wither king. The shiny, square piece of metal glowed with magical enchantments, the blood-red gem at its center glowing bright.

"The Amulet of Planes?" Watcher asked. "It's glowing so bright; what does it mean?"

"I don't know, and I don't like it." Planter's face was creased with worry. "I don't like any of this magic stuff, as I'm sure all of you know."

"We got that impression when you opened that mirror-thing in the Labyrinth." Blaster smiled at her.

Planter gave him a frown, then continued. "I can hear the Amulet whispering in my mind." She held up the Amulet of Planes. "It's saying a single word over and over."

"What's it saying?" Mapper asked.

"It's saying 'compass . . . compass . . . compass.' If it doesn't stop soon, I'm gonna go crazy." She scowled. "I hate having this voice in my mind."

"So it's just telling you to go where we were already planning on heading?" Mapper sounded confused. "That doesn't sound so terrible."

"No, that's not it." Planter put the artifact back under her armor. "Somehow, I can feel that there's something at the compass we need to find. It's pulling me toward it, and I have no option but to do what it says." She glanced at Watcher. "I hate magic. I just want to make my own choices."

"I understand, but if it's telling you to find something, maybe it'll be a weapon that can help us to bring peace." Watcher tried to sound reassuring, but he could still see the worry on Planter's beautiful face.

"Weapons rarely bring peace," Er-Lan said in a low voice. "That is, unless the peace is because everyone has been destroyed."

Everyone grew quiet as the truth of the zombie's words settled across the company.

"Our only chance to stop Krael and his withers is to form an army and fight back." Watcher glanced at Planter. "We'll go to the Compass and find this new item, then run back to the portal and return home to the Far Lands. We'll rally all the villagers there together and fight Krael where we're strong, and that's in the Far Lands."

"I like that idea." Blaster smiled excitedly. "The idea of fighting a couple of hundred withers with just us never sounded like very much fun."

"Fighting is never fun." Er-Lan shook his head, then lowered his gaze to the ground.

"Er-Lan's right, war is never fun, but we must prepare." Watcher placed a reassuring hand on the zombie's shoulder. "We need to form the largest army ever seen in Minecraft."

"An army? Like, everyone in our village?" Fencer asked.

Watcher shook his head. "I mean everyone from every village we can find. This is no longer just a contest between Krael and me."

"You mean Krael and us, don't you?" Planter added.

"Ahh . . . yeah, that's what I meant." Watcher's eyes shifted to the left and right, glancing at his companions. "This is now all-out war, and there's no prize for second place. The Great War has begun again, and if we can't stop the withers, then they might destroy everyone in the Far Lands, maybe everyone in Minecraft as well."

"Watcher's right," Cutter said. "We have no choice. Our only option is to run and hope we can get back to the portals before the withers, then go through and build an army of our own in the Far Lands."

"More soldiers usually means more violence." Er-Lan's voice was full of warning.

Watcher sighed. "I know. It's just . . . I don't know what else to do."

"I know what to do." Cutter pulled out a loaf of bread and quickly ate it. "We run and don't look back until we're in the Far Lands."

The other villagers murmured their agreement.

"Then let's go." Cutter drew his diamond sword and banged it against his chest plate. The other NPCs did the same with their weapons. "We run!"

They took off, sprinting through the ashen forest with Watcher at the rear. As he swerved around dead trees and crumbling shrubs, Watcher imagined the death and destruction Krael and his army of withers could bring upon the Far Lands, and the images he pictured in his head caused the young wizard to shake with dread.

CHAPTER 4

I t was noon when they left the dead forest, only to enter an even stranger biome. Watcher remembered this bizarre terrain from when they'd first been to the Compass. Before them, the ground fell away into a deep recession, creating a gigantic bowl spanning hundreds and hundreds of blocks. It was as if some giant leviathan had stomped its foot down upon the land, pushing on the landscape and leaving behind a massive footprint in the surface of Minecraft.

The dead forest ended at the edge of the recession where the ground sloped downward. Dead grass and bare trees gave way to a gravelly landscape, where gray, speckled blocks covered the ground, but were not the only feature to the terrain. Great arcs of stone pierced the gravel, stretching high into the air, each oriented north-to-south. Some of the arcs were small, only five or six blocks in diameter, while others stretched high into the sky. The stone curves were all across the depression like the humps of some rocky serpent breaking the surface of a gravelly ocean.

The party moved down the slope, their feet crunching on the gritty surface. As they neared the first set of granite curves, a deep humming sound, easy to feel but almost too low to hear, filled the area. The constant east-to-west wind blew through the stone rings, causing them to resonate with deep, soft tones. It made the ground vibrate slightly, the gentle tremors leaking into the villagers' feet and spreading through their bodies. Watcher thought it was an eerie feeling, as if the vibrations were reaching into his very soul.

Watcher glanced at his companions. "Can you feel it?"

They all nodded.

"I don't like it." Blaster scowled at the landscape. "I didn't like it the first time we were here, and I still don't like it."

"Don't worry; you'll be okay." Fencer put a reassuring hand on the boy's shoulder.

Blaster pushed her hand off his shoulder. "I know I'll be okay." He gave Watcher a frustrated look.

Watcher just smiled, enjoying his friend's misery.

"Let's just move faster and get out of here as soon as possible," Blaster said.

"Agreed." Watcher nodded.

Watcher led the company around the stone arcs, staying away from the larger ones that created the strongest vibrations. Ahead, the tall stone walls of the Compass loomed high into the air. The featureless wall curved around to the left and right, making a perfect circle when viewed on a map, the entire structure hundreds of blocks in diameter, the far side lost in the haze of Minecraft. In each direction of the compass, entrances pierced the rocky wall, each lined with closely spaced trees.

"I can hear a humming sound from whatever is waiting for me." Planter glanced at Watcher. "It's getting louder. I'm sure whatever is making that sound is inside the Compass."

"You lead the way," Watcher said. "That sound must mean something."

Planter nodded and shot off ahead of him, her

boots kicking up small pieces of gravel as she sprinted. Watcher tried to keep up, but she was too fast.

"Planter, slow down!" His voice echoed off the stone rings and Compass wall. "We should stay together."

But Planter ignored him and streaked onward across the landscape, passing through the Compass entrance alone. Watcher tried to go faster, but couldn't keep up; she'd always been faster than him, ever since they were young kids. He'd just have to hope she didn't go too far.

When Watcher passed through the looming wall of the Compass, the deep reverberations from the stone arcs seemed to vanish instantly. Within the walls stood a lush forest, with thick grass and the occasional flower dotting the verdant covering. Up ahead, a gigantic, dark tower stretched up into the air. It was impossibly high, with windows staring out onto the landscape like eyeless sockets. The structure was as dark as midnight; even though the sun was now nearing its zenith, the tower's surface was seemingly constructed from shadows.

"Planter . . . where are you?" Watcher shouted. He couldn't see anything other than trees.

Casting a worried glance toward Blaster and Cutter, Watcher drew the Flail of Regrets from his inventory, then grabbed a shield with his left hand. The other villagers also drew their weapons, ready for battle.

"Planter!" one of the NPCs shouted.

"Where are you?" said another.

"We should split up and look for her," Blaster said.

"No—stay together." Watcher's voice sounded more like a command than a reply. "There could be dangerous things here." He glanced at the other NPCs. "Everyone, follow me."

Watcher darted through the forest, weaving between trees and jumping over shrubs. He strained his ears trying to catch any sounds, but the Compass was completely quiet except for their footsteps. He ran faster, the silence making him more nervous.

Finally, the forest ended, revealing a large circle of

quartz on the ground. The pristine white surface was easily a hundred blocks across and looked totally out of place next to the thick and healthy forest. At the center of the quartz circle stood the dark tower, the shadowy structure in stark contrast to the lighter ground on which it stood. Redstone blocks outlined paths leading into the structure, the deep red blocks aligned with the points of the compass.

"Come on . . . she must be in there." Without waiting for a response, Watcher ran for the tower, his Flail and shield ready for battle.

But as he passed into the dark tower's shadow, he saw Planter standing at the center of the structure, staring down at the floor. When she spotted Watcher approaching and smiled at him, his fears instantly evaporated.

"It's right here." Planter pointed at the ground. "I can hear the humming coming from right here."

Watcher ran to her side, then paused to catch his breath while the rest of their companions gathered near.

"You should have waited for us," Watcher chided. "We were . . . well . . . I was afraid something might happen to you."

"I can take care of myself." She scowled.

"I know you can take care of yourself," Watcher replied. "But that doesn't stop me worrying about you."

"You're right . . . sorry." She nodded, then pointed at the ground again. "This was where we found those gauntlets on your wrists."

Watcher glanced at his wrists, where he wore ornate artifacts called the Gauntlets of Life. They were ancient, magical weapons that had saved the group a couple of times, but the cost of use was steep: they drained life from the ground on which their wielder stood, turning the landscape to petrified stone.

"There's something else down there," Planter insisted.

"We took everything out of the chest that was buried there, remember?"

"I don't care," Planter snapped. "Dig it up."

"Okay." Watcher put away his weapons and pulled out an iron pickaxe.

When she stepped back out of the way, he swung the tool at the block. Tiny little chips of quartz flew into the air, some of them stinging his cheeks and hands. After three strong blows, the cube shattered, revealing an old wooden chest . . . just as he expected. Kneeling, he opened the chest, only to find it empty.

"You see . . . it's empty." Watcher closed the lid. "I don't think there's anything here."

Planter snatched the pickaxe from Watcher's hands and shoved him out of the way, then brought the iron tool down upon the chest, smashing the ancient wooden box in only two blows. She handed him back the pick, then knelt and peered into the hole with Watcher looking over her shoulder. A passage stretched downward into the darkness, a ladder attached to one side, the rungs quickly disappearing as they descended.

"You see?!" She smiled up at him. "There's a ladder here." She stood and gave Watcher his pick. "I can still hear something humming down there; there must be a room at the end of this ladder. I think we should investigate."

Watcher stepped forward and glanced down into the dim hole. "I better go first . . . it might be dangerous."

"You know, I don't always need you to take care of me. I'm a strong and confident girl; I can take care of myself."

"No offense meant," Watcher said, stepping back. "I know you can take care of yourself, and usually you're taking care of me at the same time."

Planter smiled, then stepped into the hole, Watcher following right behind. The passage was as cold as a tomb, with an ancient feeling to it, as if time had stood still within its narrow confines for centuries. They descended for twenty or thirty blocks; it was difficult to tell. The darkness in the shaft was unusually heavy and black. It seemed to reach out to Watcher, his imagination filling the shadows with ancient monsters. Tiny, square goosebumps formed on his arms as a chill slithered down his back. He was starting to get scared.

"I'm at the end of the ladder." Planter's voice reflected off the walls, surrounding Watcher as if she were speaking to him from all sides; it felt comforting and drove away his fear.

Finally, Watcher's feet found solid ground. He glanced up the shaft. Light from the opening high overhead flickered on and off as other villagers mounted the ladder and descended.

Watcher turned and surveyed the chamber. He could tell by the echoes from his footsteps that this was a large room, but it was completely bathed in darkness, with the light from his glowing arms and chest the only thing letting him see. Two steps ahead, Planter moved cautiously into the chamber, her body invisible in the darkness, her glowing arms appearing to float in the air. She reached into her inventory and pulled out a torch, then held it high over her head, casting a wide circle of flickering light onto her surroundings. But still, the walls of the chamber remained hidden from view. She reached for another torch, but had none.

"Do you have any torches?" Planter asked.

Watcher shook his head. "Stand back. I'll make some."

Reaching into his inventory, he drew the Wand of Cloning again, the magical artifact glowing with energy. With the wand in his right hand, he waved it over his head, allowing its power to build up as it slashed at his HP, causing him to grit his teeth and stifle a shout of pain. Then he pointed it at the torch and flicked his wrist. A bright ball of light momentarily blinded Planter and Watcher. When the light faded, they found a pile of torches lying on the ground at Watcher's feet.

Planter knelt and scooped up the sticks, then held one in her hand. Instantly, it ignited, adding more light to the room. She moved throughout the chamber with Watcher on her heels, placing the torches on the ground and walls. In a minute, they'd lit the entire chamber, just as the rest of the NPCs entered the room.

Glancing at their surroundings, Watcher marveled at how old this room felt. The floor, made of stone bricks cracked with age, showed a thick layer of dust; no one had been here in a very long time. One end of the room boasted a huge fireplace, pieces of netherrack lining the bottom. Mapper moved to the hearth and struck flint to steel, lighting the rusty, speckled cubes. The flames in the fireplace spread a warm yellow glow through the room, driving out some of the chill and making it feel a little less ancient and abandoned.

"Everyone, search the chamber," Watcher said. "There must be magical artifacts hidden in here. If any of you find something, don't touch it. Wait until I can check it out."

"I better stay close to you, Blaster." Fencer's voice floated out of the darkness. A frustrated growl came from the same direction. Watcher giggled, making sure his friend would hear.

"I think I found something over here," Planter said.

She was standing near the far wall, where tall book-shelves formed a small alcove. At the center of the alcove sat an enchanting table with sparkling blue armor float-ing just above its deep red surface. Behind the enchant-ing table was an iron door with no button or lever to open it.

"I hear the humming coming from behind that door." Planter pointed to a rusted iron door at the back of the alcove.

Watcher stepped closer to the door and searched for a button or lever; there was none. He stomped on the ground, hoping to trigger a pressure plate or tripwire . . . still nothing.

Turning in frustration, he moved to the enchanting table and stared down at the strange armor floating on its velvety surface. Each deep blue piece sparkled with strange magical enchantments, though they lacked the normal iridescent purple glow that Planter's enchanted chain mail armor or Watcher's enchanted weapons possessed. Instead, bright red sparks danced across the chest plate, leggings, helmet, and boots, as if the crimson embers were somehow alive. Watcher reached down and tried to take the armor, but he couldn't lift it. Gripping the chest plate with both hands, he pulled with all his strength, but it was as if the armor was cemented to the table, unable to be moved.

"It won't budge," Watcher said. "Maybe we aren't supposed to have this armor?"

"Let me try." Planter stepped up to the enchanting table.

"You won't be able to lift it." Watcher shook his head doubtfully. "There must be some kind of enchantment holding it in place. If I couldn't move it, even with all my magical power, I doubt you'll be able to."

Planter gave him an angry scowl, then reached out and touched the sparkling blue chest plate. Instantly, a huge red spark, like a bolt of scarlet lightning, jumped from the armor and struck Planter in the chest. The blast of crimson light filled the chamber, turning night into day; it caused Watcher and the other NPCs to shut their eyes for a moment.

Planter flew backward, a shout of surprise escaping her lips. She thudded to the ground four blocks from the enchanting table, crashing into Er-Lan and Fencer, knocking them down too. Blaster rushed to Planter's side and helped her up, then reached out and offered Fencer a hand. The young girl smiled happily up at Blaster, making him cringe as he helped her to her feet.

When Watcher reached Planter's side, he found her enchanted chain mail floating on the ground beside her. The sapphire blue chest plate and leggings from the table were now wrapped around her body, hugging her tight, like a second skin. Planter glanced down at the armor and tried to pull it off, but it was firmly attached; it wasn't going anywhere.

"Does it hurt?" Watcher asked. "Is the armor causing you any pain?"

She shook her head. "Actually, it's the opposite. I feel energized."

"Perhaps this armor was meant for Planter." Er-Lan reached down and picked up Planter's old enchanted chain mail, and handed it to Fencer.

Fencer blushed, then took the armor and put it on. Blaster's eyes grew wide with surprise as the iridescent glow of the armor lit Fencer with a lavender glow, making her long blond hair stand out, as if her flowing locks were also magical. Then he turned away and smiled, embarrassed.

Watcher leaned over and picked up the dark blue helmet, ignoring the red sparks crawling across its surface like tiny red spiders. He handed it to Planter and she put it on her head, then she grabbed the boots on the ground and put them on, completing the set.

"What do you think?" Planter asked, holding her arms out and turning in a circle.

"You look beautiful, as usual." Watcher smiled.

"Look, the door is now open." Cutter pointed at the rusted iron door behind the enchanting table."

Go in. Baltheron's voice echoed in Watcher's head.

"I don't know if that's such a good idea," Watcher said aloud.

"Who are you talking to?" Blaster asked.

Watcher held up a hand, silencing his friend, then pulled out the Flail of Regrets and pointed at the iron door. "What can we expect to find in that room?"

The truth, the Flail said. *Only those with magic may hear the words from the Stone; all others enter at their own peril.*

Watcher glanced at Planter, who had a look of surprise on her beautiful face. "Did you hear?"

She nodded.

Watcher turned and faced his companions. "We must go through this door to learn something important." He paused for a moment. "All of you have to stay here."

"Sounds great," Blaster said. "That door looks a little spooky. I think I like it better out here."

"Me too." Fencer glanced at Blaster and smiled. "We can look around together."

Blaster cringed. "Maybe I'd like it better in there."

Watcher held up a hand. "No, the Flail said only Planter and I will be safe in there."

Blaster sighed.

"Stay by the fire and get warm. We'll be out as fast as possible."

The villagers murmured amongst themselves as they gathered around the roaring fire, Mapper, of course, perusing the books around the enchanting table. Watcher moved to the iron door and waited until Planter was at his side.

"I don't like the feel of this place," she said.

"Me neither." Watcher reached out and put a hand on the open door. Its surface was cold, causing an unnatural chill to spread across his skin. "I can feel the magic pulsing through this place. It's like some kind of generator for magical energy. This might not be such a good idea."

Enter or witness the destruction of Minecraft, Baltheron warned, the Flail's words deep and ominous.

Watcher glanced at Planter and saw she was feeling the same thing as him: fear.

"I guess we need . . . to go in." Her voice was soft and weak.

Watcher reached out and took her hand in his, their fingers intertwined.

"We can do this together."

"We can do *anything* together," she corrected.

He nodded, then they walked through the spooky entrance as more goosebumps spread across their bodies.

CHAPTER 5

They walked side-by-side through the narrow passage, their shoulders nearly scraping the walls. Planter's deep blue armor almost looked black in the dim corridor, but the red sparks dancing across its surface made her body seem to glow, as if she were engulfed by crimson lightning.

"I don't like the feel of this passage." Planter's voice was barely a whisper.

"What do you mean?" Watcher asked.

"Well . . . it feels like there's something waiting for us at the end of this corridor, and it knows we're coming." She glanced at her boyfriend with scared, emerald-green eyes.

"How can you tell?"

Planter stopped and turned to Watcher. "I don't know. I think I can feel the magic up ahead, and it feels . . . strange, and angry, like it's been waiting for us for a long time."

She glanced around at both ends of the passage, as if she were expecting some*one* or some*thing* to be there. "I don't like this. Magic has a way of demanding a price, like with that enchanted bow of yours."

"You mean the one I used to destroy those ancient zombie warriors in the Cave of Slumber?"

She nodded. "The same one that killed Builder . . . remember?"

Watcher nodded, a solemn expression on his square face. "You're talking about the Fossil Bow of Destruction."

Planter nodded. "I don't trust magic, and this thing we're moving toward—it knows I don't trust it."

"Well, don't worry." Watcher pulled out the Flail of Regrets, the glowing spiked ball adding to the purple light from his arms and chest. "I have lots of enchanted weapons, and they'll keep us safe."

"Great, more magic." Planter rolled her eyes, then turned and walked down the passage.

As she moved away from him, Watcher noticed a purple glow coming from Planter's upper body. Before it had been only her arms, but now the entire top half of her body was wreathed in a magical glow.

"Planter, look at your body."

Planter glanced down at herself and an expression of horror spread across her face. She immediately wiped at her chest and shoulders as if they were covered with spiders. Soon she was frantically beating at them, trying to extinguish the purple glow radiating from her body.

Watcher reached out and wrapped his arms around her. "Planter . . . it's okay. It's probably just from that new armor."

Planter stopped scratching at her arms and tried to pull off the glowing chest plate, but it held fast, as if glued to her skin.

"Why can't I get it off?" she pleaded. "I want this armor off."

"It's not a big deal; you've had enchanted armor before."

"This is different." Planter looked at him with fear in her eyes. "It's doing . . . something . . . to me. I can feel it."

"I'm sure it'll be alright. Just relax."

Planter clenched her fists and tried to calm herself. She scowled at the glowing armor. "I hate magic!"

"I know," Watcher said. "You've told me about a hundred times. But it'll be okay if we face this challenge together."

She nodded, an uncertain expression on her beautiful face, then continued down the passage with Watcher at her side.

The hallway finally ended in a square room about a dozen blocks on a side. The light from redstone lanterns positioned in the corners cast a warm orange glow on the chamber. The stone walls were featureless and smooth, but the floor was a mosaic of different types of blocks: gravel, diorite, granite, and andesite, each one a different color and texture, creating a quilt-like appearance. At the center of the room stood a glass altar with a dark purple cloth covering something sitting on top.

Watcher reached out to grab the dark cloth. A bright spark jumped from the cloth to his hand, making his fingers momentarily numb. The covering now sparkled with magical energy, just like his magical weapons. Grabbing a corner, he pulled the cloth off the altar, revealing a round obsidian stone. It was completely smooth, and its curved surface looked unnatural to both of them.

Touch the Memory Stone. Baltheron's voice whispered in their minds.

Watcher threw the shimmering cloth over a shoulder, then glanced at Planter and nodded. Both moved closer to the altar and laid their hands on the stone.

"During the Great War, the wizards planned for this day," a deep voice rumbled, making the walls and floors shake ever so slightly as the sound came at them from all sides. "The Wizard of War and the Wizard of Peace have met again, and the bond between you is strong, just as predicted."

"What are you saying?" Watcher asked.

"No questions . . . just listen," the voice replied. "I am the Memory Stone, put here to help the Wizards of War and Peace in their hour of need."

"What are you talking about?" Watcher asked.

Planter laid a finger on his lips, silencing him. "Just listen."

"The Wizard of Peace is wise," the Memory Stone said.

Planter smiled proudly.

"The wizards built the Hall of Planes and the portals to connect all the worlds of Minecraft together." The Memory Stone's voice thundered through the chamber, making the ground vibrate. "They used a Crown of Skulls as bait to lure the withers to this world and into the Cave of Slumber. But the wizards added another secret, unbeknownst to villager or monster: any creature trying to leave this world through those portals will die."

"What?!" Watcher started to pull his hand away from the stone's smooth surface, but Planter placed hers on top of his, calming him.

"Just listen," she said calmly.

Watcher sighed, then nodded.

The stone continued. "This was to ensure the withers could never escape. But you can still go back to your world if each person carries a portal key."

"You mean like this one?" Planter reached under her armor and pulled out the Amulet of Planes, which she'd found in the Wizard's Tower many weeks ago. The shiny square of metal reflected the light from the redstone lanterns, the blood-red gem at the center glowing with magical power.

Watcher, somehow, felt the stone nod in agreement.

"The portal keys have been hidden with the strongest weapons created by the great wizards." The Memory Stone's words quickened, the volume getting louder, as if the mind trapped within its smooth surface was getting excited. "They are held securely in the Weapons

Vault. But only one person still knows the location of the Vault."

The Stone's voice slowed and grew softer. "You must find the last surviving wizard from the Great War, Mirthrandos. That wizard can take you to the Weapons Vault and help you to escape back to your own plane of existence within the Server Pyramid."

"How do we find Mirthrandos?" Planter asked.

"Yeah, how do we find him?" Watcher added.

"Their location is protected," the memory stone said. "To find Mirthrandos, you must solve these two riddles:

"First: I have arms but have no strength. When you wave at me, I always wave back . . . What am I?

"And second: I am not alive. I have no mouth, yet I devour everything. I have no lungs, but need air to survive. I cannot drink, but water will kill me."

The stone paused for a moment, letting the riddles sink in, then continued. "Find the place where both exist in harmony, and you will find Mirthrandos."

The stone grew quiet. Watcher and Planter waited for it to say more, but instead, they felt its magical presence leave the room; they were alone.

"What is Mirthrandos?" a voice asked from behind.

Startled, Planter and Watcher both jumped, then turned to find Er-Lan standing in the chamber, staring at them.

"What are you doing in here?" Watcher asked. "The magic in this room could have hurt you!"

"Er-Lan seems unharmed," the zombie replied, looking around doubtfully.

"I know, but you shouldn't have taken that risk." Watcher moved to the monster's side, then gently pushed him from the room. "Let's all get out of here before that Memory Stone decides to blast us with magic."

"I agree," Planter said. "This place gives me the creeps, especially that stone. There aren't even any *corners* on it. That makes no sense!"

The trio quickly left the room as the redstone

lanterns behind them grew dimmer and dimmer until they shut off, plunging the chamber and passage into complete darkness. They had to rely on the purple glow coming from Watcher's and Planter's arms and chest, along with the red sparks from Planter's new armor, which added a crimson hue.

As they walked, Watcher glanced over his shoulder at the darkened chamber. For some reason, he had the feeling the Memory Stone had not told them everything. There was something being held back, and whatever it was . . . it was dangerous.

CHAPTER 6

Watcher stepped out of the passage and into the tiny alcove, the dark purple cloth sparkling on his shoulder. Nearby, Mapper stood next to the bookshelves surrounding the enchanting table, looking at the spine of every book and pulling some off the shelves to peruse their contents. Watcher stepped past the old man and moved to Blaster and Cutter.

"Well . . . you seem to be still alive." Blaster smiled. "I'm guessing your little adventure in the scary tunnel was successful?"

The rest of the NPCs gathered around him.

Watcher nodded. "We learned some interesting things in there."

"Yeah, like the fact that anyone going through the portal to get back home will die." Anger and frustration filled Planter's voice. "The magic of those portals has a hidden price."

"We can't go home?" Fencer asked.

"We have to stay in this terrible place?" Cutter sounded as disappointed as Fencer.

"No." Watcher shook his head, then frowned at Planter. "That's not the whole story. If we each carry a portal key like the one Planter has, then we'll be okay."

He gestured for her to show the Amulet of Planes to the others. She reached under her dark blue armor and withdrew the necklace, the magical artifact hanging from its impossibly thin silver chain. She held it out for everyone to see.

"That's a portal key?" Mapper asked. He moved closer to it, glancing at the glowing gem at the center of the reflective square.

"Yep," Planter said as she put it back under her dark-blue armor.

"We just need to get a bunch of those amulets, and then we'll be fine." Watcher smiled as if he had it all figured out.

"That's great and all," Blaster said. "But where do we get those keys? You have 'em in your pocket?"

"Well . . . no." Watcher shook his head.

"But whatever gave you this insight, back there in that scary tunnel, it told you where to find the keys, right?" Blaster frowned as if he already knew the answer.

"Well . . . no, we don't know where they are."

"This is great!" Blaster's sarcasm caused some to chuckle, while others frowned with concern.

"We did learn something about their location," Planter added.

"Finally, something useful." Blaster turned to her. "What did you learn?"

"It's a riddle." Planter pointed to Watcher. "Tell them."

"A riddle? That's what's gonna help us get home before the withers reach the Far Lands?" Cutter's frustrated voice boomed through the chamber. The big NPC faced Watcher and gave him an impatient glare.

"Well, first of all, the Memory Stone told us—"

"You were talking to a stone in there?" Blaster asked. Watcher nodded.

"Let him finish," Cutter said, silencing Blaster's sarcastic comment before it escaped his lips.

"There is a wizard still left in this world. His name is

Mirthrandos, and he knows the location of the Weapons Vault. In the Vault, we'll find the portal keys." Watcher waited for everyone to process what he was saying. "All we need to do is find Mirthrandos, and he'll take us to the Vault."

"*If* Mirthrandos is a 'he,'" Er-Lan added. "This zombie never heard the stone say 'he.' Perhaps 'he' is a 'she.'"

"I doubt that," Watcher said. "The Stone gave us a riddle to help us find the great Mirthrandos."

"So what's the riddle?" Mapper asked excitedly. "I was always good at riddles. One time, when I was young, someone asked—"

"Mapper . . . later, okay?" Planter put a hand on the old man's shoulder.

He nodded and turned his good ear toward Watcher, ready to listen.

"Okay, the first riddle is this: 'I have arms but have no strength. When you wave at me, I always wave back . . . What am I?'

"And the second one is: 'I am not alive. I have no mouth, yet I devour everything. I have no lungs, but need air to survive. I cannot drink, but water will kill me.'

"If we can figure out where the answers to these two riddles exist—together—then we'll find Mirthrandos."

They stood in silence, each villager wracking their brains, trying to figure out the answers.

"The first is obvious." Er-Lan glanced at Watcher and gave him a toothy smile.

"What do you mean?" Planter asked.

"It is a reflection." The zombie glanced around at the other companions. They just stared back at him, confused. Er-Lan moved his arms through the air. "Arms but no strength . . . wave and it always waves back . . . it is a reflection."

"Of course, a reflection. Good going, Er-Lan." Mapper patted the zombie on the back.

"Ok, so we're looking for some kind of reflection."

Watcher glanced at the zombie. "What about the second riddle?"

"Er-Lan has thought about that, but no ideas come to this zombie's head."

Watcher sighed, then glanced at Mapper. The old man shook his head as well.

"Anyone understand the second riddle?" Watcher asked.

"Say it again. Maybe I'll figure it out the second time, 'cause I'm so smart." Blaster gave the NPCs a sarcastic grin, making them all chuckle.

"Okay. 'I am not alive. I have no mouth, yet I devour everything. I have no lungs, but need air to survive. I cannot drink, but water will kill me.'" Watcher stared at Blaster, hoping he'd come up with something.

The boy shrugged after a moment. "Sorry, but I got nothin'."

"Anyone else?" Watcher turned, glancing at the other villagers.

"We need to figure this out." Blaster's smile turned to a scowl. "Everyone . . . think!"

"Well," a soft voice said. "It seems kinda obvious to me." Everyone turned and looked at Fencer. "It's fire . . . right?"

"No mouth, but I devour everything. No lungs, but I need air." Watcher nodded his head and smiled. "Can't drink, but water will kill me . . . of course! It's fire!"

"Great job, Fencer," Blaster said. Fencer gave him a gigantic smile, her whole face lighting up with joy. She took a step toward him.

"Oh no." Blaster quickly retreated, the rest of the NPCs laughing.

"So, we need to find a place where there's fire and a reflection all at the same time," Mapper said.

"The only place I've ever seen a reflection in Minecraft is in a pool of water," Cutter said. "Maybe there's some kind of pond or river that's on fire."

"That doesn't sound very likely," Watcher said, feeling doubtful.

"Check the map." Planter glanced at Mapper. The old man pulled out the magical map and stared down at it. The ancient parchment showed the Cave of Slumber, with the Creeper's Teeth along the bottom.

Planter reached out and touched the fragile paper. A bright red spark jumped from her finger and danced across the map, making the features change. Instantly, it showed the Compass at the center, strange biomes around the edges.

Watcher reached out with a hand and placed two fingers on the map, then pinched them together. Instantly, the map zoomed out, showing a larger area.

"What's that?" Planter pointed to a red and blue circle, then touched it.

Instantly, the map zoomed in on the circle, enlarging the image and revealing writing around the object.

Mapper held the map up to his aged eyes. "It says 'Lake of Fire' I think." He moved it closer to his wrinkled face. "The writing is very faint, but I'm pretty sure that's right."

"Lake of Fire?" Watcher said. "That sounds like where we need to go to find this Mirthrandos."

"And when we find him, we'll find the portal keys?" Cutter asked, his voice booming throughout the chamber.

Watcher nodded. "That's the plan."

"Then let's get moving," the big warrior said. "It looks to be due west of the Compass. We can just follow the setting sun. It shouldn't take more than half a day to get there."

The other villagers nodded and started to move, but Blaster stopped them. "Wait a minute."

They stopped and glanced at the young boy.

"What's the problem?" Cutter asked, impatient.

"I want to know what's going on with the cape thing on Watcher's shoulder." Blaster pointed at the dark purple cloth hanging on Watcher's shoulder. It shimmered and sparkled with magical energy.

"This? Well . . . it was covering the Memory Stone." Watcher held it out with both hands. "I figured since it was sparkling with magical enchantments, I should keep it."

"Just what you need—more magical stuff." Planter scowled.

"It's okay; I'm a powerful wizard, and should be able to take care of this." Watcher grinned as many of the NPCs rolled their eyes at his boast. "I have lots of magical weapons, after all."

"Here we go again," Blaster said.

Many of the NPCs giggled.

"What does it do?" Mapper asked, curious.

It is the Cape of Tharus, Baltheron said in Watcher's mind. *It was the symbol of his authority as the greatest wizard in the land. Put it on.*

"You think I should?" Watcher sounded uncertain.

"Oh no, he's talking to his toys again." Blaster gave him a sarcastic smile.

Put it on. Baltheron's urgent voice boomed through his head.

Watcher swung the cape over his head and tied it to the shoulders of his chest plate. It hung down his back, just barely touching the floor, the edges sparkling with power. "Now I look like a real wizard."

"Oh boy." Blaster shook his head. "This is really gonna help his ego."

"You can be sure of that," Cutter said. "The last thing we need is a wizard with an ego."

"Hey . . . this cape belonged to the greatest wizard ever, Tharus." Watcher walked around, allowing the cape to flow behind him, looking like a wave of magic. He glanced over his shoulder and smiled in satisfaction. "Since I'm the most powerful wizard here, it makes sense I should wear it." He glanced at Planter.

"Whatever." She looked disgusted with him.

Watcher glanced at Blaster and Cutter. Both just shook their heads, expressions of disbelief on their square faces.

"I think the cape is pretty," Fencer said.

"It's not pretty, it's powerful." Watcher sounded offended.

"Well, *I* think it's pretty."

Blaster chuckled, causing the other villagers to laugh too.

"Hey!" Watcher complained, but no one listened to him.

"Come on, pretty wizard, let's find that lake of fire." Blaster laughed again, causing more chuckles to fill the chamber.

Watcher waited for the rest to go, then headed for the ladder. He found Planter waiting for him, a look of annoyance on her face.

"Oh no . . . what did I do this time?" he asked.

"Oh . . . you . . . nothing, this time." She sounded angry. "It's just, did you see the map react to me?"

"Sure," Watcher replied. "It was your magic that made the map change, just like it does for me."

Planter just frowned.

"I don't understand . . . this is a good thing." Watcher gave her a smile, hoping to ease her worries. It didn't work.

"I don't know." Planter's brow creased with uncertainty. "Magic didn't seem to help this world very much. Will it really help us, or just do more damage? It always has a hidden price; what will it demand of me?"

"You worry too much." Watcher reached out and took her hand in his. "What harm could magic really do? We'll get these portal keys, then be out of this world. When we're in the Far Lands, we can prepare for the withers."

"I guess . . . I just don't trust magic. I hate it."

"I know," Watcher replied. "But I'll be there to take care of you and keep you safe."

"I hope so," Planter said. "I'm relying on you . . . don't let me down."

She turned and climbed the ladder. As Watcher grabbed the rungs, he hoped he hadn't just lied to her. Planter was right; magic had a way of doing what it wanted, and sometimes, it was dangerous—really dangerous—to be near.

"I'll do my best, Planter," Watcher whispered as he climbed the ladder. "I'll do my best."

CHAPTER 7

Krael floated down the slopes of the huge mountains, the rest of his army following close behind. With the thin sliver of the moon high overhead doing little to light the surroundings, the withers relied upon the silvery glow of the twinkling stars to make the steep sides of the Creeper's Teeth visible.

Fortunately, the floating monsters had incredible night vision; they had no trouble finding innocent monsters with which to sate their thirst for violence. The withers' flaming skulls were like lethal hail as they bombarded the horrific monsters inhabiting the Teeth. The creatures populating the mountains were a mixture of different body parts: skeleton heads on zombies, endermen with zombie arms, and spiders with blaze heads. The withers attacked them not because they were a threat, which they weren't; rather, they destroyed the horrific monsters simply because they could. Frequently, laughter would echo off the sandy mountains as the withers enjoyed their game to the detriment of their targets.

"Husband, do we head for the Far Lands? Many are excited about exacting revenge upon the NPCs." Kora's three heads had kind expressions on their dark faces, but Krael knew those innocent looks were deceiving; she was a vicious fighter.

"That's what the wizards want us to do," Krael said with an evil sneer. "But I know the secret of the portals that those pathetic wizards hid from so many for so long."

"Secret?" Kora asked, her curious voice soft and soothing.

Krael launched a pair of flaming skulls at a spidery-looking creature with a dozen legs, if not more—the dark appendages sticking out from the large, gelatinous body of a slime. The spider-slime's lime-colored face turned from angry to terrified when it spotted the deadly projectiles. The spider-slime tried to scuttle away, but the flaming skulls blasted it, taking all of its HP.

"Nice shot, dear." Kora's three skulls spoke in unison.

Krael beamed with pride.

"I love how much imagination the wizards put into populating the slopes of the Creeper's Teeth. The creatures are so interesting. It's too bad for the wizards these monsters are no threat to us." Kora threw a flaming skull at a tiny wolf with a skeleton's head in the distance, but the creature saw the projectile coming and dashed into a nearby cave, avoiding the attack. She laughed. "Still not as good as you."

Krael said nothing, just nodded.

"Now, what were you saying, something about a secret?" she said.

"Yes, the secret about the portals." Krael glanced over his shoulder. His army was flowing over the Creeper's Teeth like a gloomy wave, their dark bodies blotting out the star-speckled sky and the slim, crescent-shaped moon. "The wizards built the Hall of Planes and the portals to draw our people into this world. But what they never revealed was that the portals only work one way—coming *into* this world."

"What do you mean, husband?" Kora asked.

"If someone tries to leave this world through those

portals, the magical enchantments built into the door-ways will kill them."

"You mean we're trapped here?" one of the withers asked.

"I thought we'd get to destroy the Far Lands," another hissed angrily.

"Be calm, my brothers and sisters," Krael said, the three Crowns of Skulls on his head glowing bright, bands of magical energy flowing from one to another, forming an iridescent halo that hugged his ashen skulls. "We will have our revenge, I promise you. While all of you slept in your prison these past centuries, I struggled to free you."

"How . . . what did you do?" a wither demanded, an accusatory tone to its scratchy voice.

Krael glared at the disrespectful monster, the Crowns growing bright with power. Fear spread across the offending wither's face, and the creature lowered his gaze, slowly descending closer to the ground.

"I read," the king of the withers said. "The foolish wizards tried to keep their secrets, but they couldn't help showing off by writing everything they knew in books. I found one of their libraries and read everything I could find. That's how I found the first Crown of Skulls." Krael smiled triumphantly.

"These books hinted that gold might awaken you from your forced slumber, so the wither king before me, Kaza, took my suggestion and tried to raise a mountain of gold, but that idiotic boy-wizard interrupted our plans."

Krael slowed to a stop and hovered in mid-air, allowing many of the withers to catch up and move closer. "I then tried to gather an army of skeletons to distract the NPCs while I had spiders make potions that would awaken you, but the boy-wizard got in the way again." Krael's left skull hissed and his right skull's eyes glowed bright with rage. "But I also found a book written by the wizard, Janus, who constructed the Hall of Planes and the portals leading to all the different worlds. That fool revealed the secret about the portals."

He paused as the rest of the wither army finally moved off the Teeth's slopes and came closer.

"We cannot go through those portals without dying, but—"

"Then what are we going to do?"

"How do we get back to the Far Lands?"

"When will we have our revenge?"

A barrage of questions bombarded Krael as the fears within many of the withers finally boiled to the surface. An annoyed look came over the wither king as he waited for silence, but the monsters kept asking their questions, fear and uncertainty ruling their minds.

"BE QUIET!" Krael's voice boomed like thunder, amplified by the three Crowns.

He glared at his army, his eyes filled with dangerous rage. Krael wanted to strike out at one of them, teaching them the danger of questioning the king of the withers.

"Husband, I know you have a plan." Kora's voice was a soothing breeze, cooling the flames of rage burning within him.

The anger in Krael's eyes dimmed as he glanced at his wife. "You're right, Kora, I do have a plan." Krael smiled at her, then turned to his army of withers. "The foolish wizard, Janus, wrote how to get past the deadly enchantments in the portals." The wither army was now completely quiet, every pair of eyes focused on their king. "They left portal keys in the Weapons Vault."

"But the Weapons Vault is in Wizard City," a wither said. "No one knows where that City is hidden."

"That is true, brother," Krael said. "No one knows where Wizard City lies in this world."

The king of the withers smiled.

"You know where it is, don't you, husband?" Kora's voice was filled with pride.

"I don't know exactly where it is," Krael said, "but I have the clue that will lead us there. We just need to figure out what the clue means."

"What is the clue?" Kora asked.

"The clue is in the form of a riddle." Krael's three heads looked around, making sure all were listening. "It goes like this: 'With feathers I fly, yet I have no wings. My body is straight and true, and my head razor-sharp. I can be held in the palm of your hand, yet never thrown.' We must figure out what this means, and then it will lead us to Wizard City."

The withers glanced at each other, trying to figure out the clue.

"I'm sure one of you will figure it out, but while we wait, we will raise an army of monsters and prepare for the Great War that we'll unleash upon the Far Lands. There are many monsters here in this world who remember the Great War and will come to our aid. We will move across the landscape, finding recruits. Either they will join our cause or be destroyed."

Kora smiled and nodded, the rest of the withers doing the same.

"Come, my brothers and sisters; we have a world to conquer." Krael laughed, then floated away from the Creeper's Teeth, hunting for allies—or victims.

He didn't really care which.

CHAPTER 8

Watcher sprinted as fast as he could, his sparkling purple cape flapping behind him as they raced the moon to the western horizon. Stars sparkled overhead in the cloudless night sky, the glittering lights looking like rare gems sewn into the dark heavens. The stone rings played their deep, sad sounds as the wind blew through their granite arcs. The vibrations slowly worked on the NPCs' nerves, making each of them nervous and jumpy. The crescent moon high overhead offered little of its silvery light to illuminate their surroundings, adding to the eerie environment.

"That cape looks ridiculous on you," Planter said in a low voice.

Watcher glanced over his shoulder and found her right behind him. "This cape belonged to Tharus. Who knows what it can do for my magical powers?"

Planter moved next to him, then shook her head. "You aren't Tharus; you're Watcher. It's like you're trying to be something you're not."

"I'm a wizard, just like Tharus." Watcher turned away from her and stared straight ahead. He reached into his inventory, his fingers bumping against the Elytra wings from his sister. He pushed them aside, then drew

Needle with his left hand, the Flail of Regrets with his right. "I have all these magical weapons and the power to use them, just like a real wizard."

"Just because a weapon is in hand does not mean it needs to be used," Er-Lan said from behind.

"Our zombie friend is right." Planter glanced over her shoulder and gave the zombie a smile, then turned back to Watcher. "Be the wielder . . . not the weapon."

"You just don't understand." He scowled at his girl-friend, then sprinted ahead, leaving her and Er-Lan behind.

Finally, the stone rings receded behind them as the party climbed a gravelly slope and entered a strange forest. Huge oak and birch trees filled the forest, stretching up to the clouds, their trunks two to three blocks wide, their different barks creating a striped background. Watcher stared up at the leafy foliage in wonder—the branches of the tallest trees were lost in the clouds. Long blades of grass swayed in the perpetual east-to-west wind, hiding colorful flowers of red and green, with mushrooms peeking up through the wavering green stalks. It was a serene environment with the constant rumble of the vibrating stone rings finally gone; each villager breathed a sigh of relief.

As they moved between the gigantic trees, the sounds of animal life began percolating through the forest, coming at them from all sides. Chickens clucked, cows mooed, sheep bleated and pigs oinked; all added to the noise, filling the forest with the sounds of life, but for some reason they couldn't see any of the creatures. The animal noises seemed to move around their party as if the mysterious creatures were surrounding the intruders, yet the villagers couldn't see any of them . . . the sound of the animals' footsteps strangely absent as well.

"You notice we can't see any of the animals?" Watcher whispered to Blaster, the lack of any visible creatures making him want to keep his voice low.

"Yeah, but I'm sure it's no big deal." Blaster patted Watcher on the back reassuringly. "Haven't you ever been moving through the woods in the Far Lands and heard animals, but didn't see them?"

"Sure, in the jungle or maybe in a dense forest." Watcher glanced around, looking for the owner of a recent loud moo. "But here, there's nothing blocking our view. All the tree branches are way up there." He pointed to the leafy canopy high overhead. He lowered his voice a little more. "We should be able to see these animals. It doesn't make sense, and that makes me worry a little."

"There's no need to be concerned," Cutter said. Obviously, the big NPC had been listening. "The withers are far from here, and they have no idea where we're going. You worry too much."

"I just want to be prepared," Watcher said. "Who knows what kind of traps the wizards or warlocks could have left around here?"

"There you go, letting all that magic stuff go to your head." Cutter drew his blade. "I let my sword do the worrying for me. All the rest takes care of itself."

"I wish I had your confidence, but I'm responsible for everyone here; I have to worry." Watcher adjusted his diamond armor, then pulled the Flail of Regrets from his inventory, the spiked cube, chain and leather-wrapped handle all glowing bright with magical energy. Glancing to the left and right, he slowed and walked next to Planter. "Do you feel anything . . . you know . . . strange?"

She nodded. "Yeah, I can feel something. It's like there's a presence out there, watching me. It's just at the edge of my senses, but I can't tell what it is." She stared at him, looking unhappy. "I hate feeling something magical out there, stalking us . . . waiting for something."

"Don't worry; we can take care of it with our own magic." Watcher reached out and took her hand in his. "We'll face it together."

"Your overconfidence in *our* magic is a problem." Planter scowled. "You don't even understand your own magic, much less mine. And now you expect me to help protect everyone using powers I can't comprehend." She sighed and looked away. "I hate magic."

Suddenly, the animal sounds around them disappeared, as if the invisible creatures just vanished. The forest became unusually silent, with the rustling of the leaves high overhead and the villagers' footsteps the only audible sounds.

Watcher continued running forward across the dim forest floor, his eyes searching the terrain for threats. At times, he ran backward, checking to make sure nothing was trying to sneak up on them.

"You okay?" Blaster asked.

The voice startled Watcher. He turned forward again and glanced at his friend. "I feel like something's watching us."

"I know; I feel it too." Blaster drew his two curved knives, his black leather armor helping him melt into the darkness. "There's something out there, and I don't like it."

Mapper moved next to Watcher. "Did you see those tiny pools of water next to the bases of the trees?" The old man pointed to a massive oak. Holes two blocks by two blocks in size sat near the trunk of the tree, each filled with water. "Why do you think those are there?"

Watcher shrugged. "I don't know." He glanced around and saw many more of the small pools of water all throughout this part of the forest, each positioned near the base of a massive tree. "It is kinda strange. Maybe it's for—"

"Monsters!" Er-Lan shouted suddenly. "There is an attack!"

Everyone stopped running and glanced at the zombie. Er-Lan's green skin looked pale as he glanced around, searching for threats.

"Er-Lan, where are the monsters?" Cutter asked.

The zombie just shook his head. "Horrible things . . . horrible things come."

"Everyone, form a circle." Watcher drew the Flail of Regrets, then pulled out an ordinary wooden shield. He moved next to Planter, her emerald green eyes filled with fear.

"Look . . . I can see the Lake of Fire," Mapper said, pointing toward the setting moon. In the distance, a lake reflected the moonlight, its rippling surface covered with fire. "Let's head for it."

"No—Er-Lan said there were monsters coming." Watcher glanced at the zombie, whose scarred face was creased with fear. "He's never been wrong about these things before. We wait until it's safe."

"I don't see any monsters," Cutter said. "Maybe Er-Lan thought—"

A loud splash came from off to the left, a spray of water flying high into the air as if something heavy had fallen from above and landed in the pool. Another splash happened to the right, then a barrage of splashes broke the quiet all around the companions. As the misty spray from each settled, strange, horrific monsters stepped from the water and growled. The creatures were pieced together from various types of monsters—a zombie head on a skeleton, a slime with spider legs, an enderman with zombie arms; each of them was different and terrifying. The splashes continued as more of the monsters leapt from the treetops and landed in the pools of water, adding to the growling army.

"We can't stay here; there are too many of them." Watcher glanced at his companions. "Head for the Lake of Fire."

Watcher sprinted straight for a group of monsters blocking his path. Swinging the Flail over his head, he filled it with magical power, then struck, the ancient weapon glowing bright. The spiked ball smashed into the terrible creatures, flinging them to the side, each flashing red as they took damage. Behind Watcher,

Planter's bow sang as flaming arrows streaked through the air, hitting monster after monster. Blaster ran out amongst the horrific creatures, slashing at them with razor-sharp knives as he dashed by, his black leather armor making him hard to see. The monsters tried to close in from behind, but they were too slow.

The villagers had escaped the trap, avoiding becoming surrounded, but now the NPCs had a monster horde pursuing them, and ahead was the massive Lake of Fire. As they neared, Watcher saw thick bushes and closely packed trees near the left and right sides of the lake; there was no escape in those directions. They were trapped with the Lake of Fire ahead and a huge army of terrifying monsters behind.

Watcher skidded to a stop near the edge of the lake and faced his friends. "We need to make a stand here. Everyone, place blocks of stone on the ground to give yourself some protection."

Watcher put away the Flail and shield and extended his arms, the magical Gauntlets of Life glowing on each wrist. He moved toward the approaching mob, despite their snarling growls filling the air. The creatures slowed as Watcher came forward, his glowing arms and torso likely giving them pause.

"Watcher, what are you doing?" Mapper shouted.

The young wizard glanced over his shoulder. "I'm gonna use the Gauntlets of Life. All of you stay back."

Just then, a monster larger than any he'd ever seen stepped forward. It was a huge, charged creeper, easily twice the size of a normal one. Sheets of blue lightning wrapped around the creature like electric armor, crackling and charging the air; it made the hairs on Watcher's arms stand up. The monster stared at him and smiled evilly, then slowly approached.

"That's a charged creeper!" Blaster shouted. "Their explosions are huge; you'll never survive that blast. If those Gauntlets can't stop him, you'll be in some serious trouble."

I have to keep my friends safe, Watcher thought. *I can do this with our magic.*

Watcher glanced over his shoulder. He could see scared expressions on all of their faces, but the one most important to him was his girlfriend. "Planter, come help me."

But the girl stayed put, a look of terror on her beautiful face.

"Okay then, I'll take care of this myself." He turned and faced the huge charged creeper, the sound of crackling sparks filling the air. "Come on, creeper, let's do this."

The huge creeper charged, a stubby-toothed smile on its mottled face; it was completely unafraid. And at that moment, Watcher wondered if this would be his last battle . . . ever.

CHAPTER 9

The charged creeper let out a high-pitched screech, then started its ignition process as it neared, its body glowing brighter and brighter, casting a harsh glare on the dark forest. Watcher extended the Gauntlets and glanced at the ground, making sure he was standing on something alive, then gathered his magic and readied an attack.

Suddenly, a loud "NO!" pierced the air.

Planter rushed to his side, her red shield covered with purple flames. She stepped in front of him, then lunged toward the creeper. The iridescent shield shot out a pulse of magical power, shoving the charged creeper backward. Swelling as it flew backward, the creeper grew brighter, then exploded as it landed on its back amidst the monster horde. The blast tore into the forest floor, turning the ground into a fiery crater as the creeper's explosion enveloped the other monsters. More than half of the mob was destroyed by the giant creeper, leaving the rest disoriented.

Watcher glanced at Planter, about to say *thank you,* but the horrified expression on her face kept him silent. More monsters fell from the trees as those who survived the explosion climbed snarling to their feet, looks of hatred in their lifeless eyes.

Looking over his shoulder, Watcher checked on his friends. They each had weapons out, ready to fight. He reached into his inventory and pulled out the Flail of Regrets and held it over his head. "Everyone . . . charge!"

Swinging the flail over his head, Watcher sprinted toward the surviving monsters.

"Planter, use your bow," Watcher shouted over his shoulder, but no arrows fell upon the monsters.

Blaster streaked by, a strangely gleeful laugh coming from the boy as he sped through the enemy formation, slashing at them with his curved knives as he passed. Cutter smashed into a group of spider-zombies, whose green heads looked out of place on their fuzzy black bodies. The big NPC attacked the monsters, his diamond sword cleaving a path of destruction.

Watcher struck a tall skeleton with the Flail, sending the creature flying through the air to land on the ground with a thud. Not waiting for the monster to get up or retrieve his dropped bow, Watcher attacked the monster again, the Flail devouring the last of the creature's HP.

As Watcher swung his flail at creature after creature, trying to protect his friends, the rest of the NPCs fell into combat around him, the villagers fighting in pairs, each one watching the other's back. Shouts of pain and fear filled the air, some from the villagers, but mostly from the monsters. The terrible creatures fought without any thought of surrender or retreat. It was almost as if they were fighting the Great War again, and that had Watcher concerned.

The young wizard smashed a zombie with his flail, then rolled across the ground just as a skeleton with an enderman head fired an arrow at him. He took the creature's bony legs out from under it, then brought the flail down upon the monster, shattering its HP.

Suddenly, the sound of watery splashes filled the air

again; monster reinforcements were coming. Watcher turned to look for the new creatures when a sharp claw tore into his forearm, making him drop the Flail of Regrets.

He drew Needle and slashed at the fuzzy black spider that had attacked. The monster had what seemed like a dozen legs, each tipped with a wicked, curved claw. Watcher backed away from the creature as the sounds of more monster footsteps filled the air.

We're losing this battle, Watcher thought sadly.

Use the Gauntlets, a mean and scratchy voice said in his mind.

He glanced down at the Gauntlets of Life on each wrist, the metallic artifacts pulsing with power.

"I have to do it." Watcher glanced at his friends, then checked the ground; he was standing on grass, with clumps of bushes nearby . . . good. "Everyone back up!"

The NPCs kept fighting.

"EVERYONE BACK UP!" Watcher's voice boomed through the forest, amplified by his magic.

The villagers and monsters, both shocked by the deafening sound, stopped fighting for just an instant. That gave the NPCs a chance to retreat, leaving Watcher standing before the enemy horde, alone.

Before any of the creatures could move, Watcher threw every ounce of power he had into the magical gauntlets. The artifacts grew brighter and brighter, the iridescent light pushing back on the darkness and turning the night into a lavender-hued day. He extended his arms toward the mob, then released his power and let it flow. Purple bolts of lightning flew from his hands and engulfed the monsters. The creatures screamed, their warped mouths filled with wails of agony, as the shafts of energy burned away at their HP.

Watcher moved forward, sending more sheets of purple electricity stabbing at the creatures, while under his feet, the grass-covered ground turned to stone, the thin, green blades turning gray and brittle. The petrified grass crunched underfoot as he advanced, throwing more bolts of iridescent death at the monsters.

The creatures tried to flee, running into the forest, but Watcher kept firing. Behind him, a villager yelled something, but he didn't hear; he was completely focused on the destruction of the monster horde.

Eventually, someone grabbed his arm and shook him gently, then not-so-gently, yelling loud as they almost knocked him to the ground.

He stopped the flow of magic as the words registered . . . it was Planter's voice.

"STOP . . . let them go!" Her voice shook with anger. "Watcher, let them—"

"Ok, I stopped." He lowered his arms, but kept his eyes on the retreating monsters. Only a few had survived; it made Watcher grin.

"What are you smiling about?!"

Watcher pointed. "I was able to destroy most of the monsters and chase the rest away." He glanced at the other NPCs, expecting congratulations or cheers, but instead, he saw horrified expressions on all their faces except Cutter's. The big warrior nodded at Watcher with an expression of pride on his face.

"You attacked those monsters when they tried to run away." Planter stared at him as if he were some kind of monster. "You didn't need to do that. You didn't need to destroy them . . . you could have let them flee."

"And have them come back when they have more troops? I don't think so." Watcher moved to where he dropped the Flail of Regrets and picked it up. "I only did what was necessary to protect everyone."

"I don't think so," she said, hands clenched into fists.

"What do you mean?"

"You looked like you enjoyed it, regardless of the cost." Planter pointed at the ground. "Look what you did to this forest."

Watcher glanced down. A huge circle of petrified grass surrounded him, marking where the Gauntlets had siphoned life from the grass and ground, using it to power their magical enchantments. The stone circle also enveloped a group of bushes, as well as a cluster of tall birch trees, whose pristine white bark was now a pale gray. The fabric of Minecraft around him felt empty and dead, having paid the price the Gauntlets of Life demanded.

"Look at what your magic has done." Planter scowled, anger simmering behind her deep green eyes.

"Yeah . . . I see." Watcher turned and faced her. "My magic saved everyone and chased away the monsters. Sure, it did some damage to the land, but I'd rather hurt some grass than see a friend injured."

"But you couldn't stop destroying those monsters. You had a crazed look on your face when I finally shook some sense into you." She turned away from him. "If I hadn't stopped you, I bet you would have killed all of them."

"Good!" Cutter shouted. "Let 'em be destroyed . . . who needs 'em?"

"Killing should be the last solution to any problem." Er-Lan moved next to Planter, placing his scarred, green hand on her shoulder. "Once the enemy is in retreat, violence should stop."

"But what if they come back?" The big warrior's feet crunched the petrified blades of grass as he approached. "I say kill the monsters now, then none of them will come back."

"That's the same kind of thinking some of the NPC wizards used during the Great War," Mapper said. "Many of the wizards claimed to be protecting Minecraft by trying to exterminate the monsters. They didn't want the monsters to become greater threats, so they tried to destroy them all. Many of the books I've read suggest this kind of thinking led to the spread of the Great War across multiple planes of existence."

"You mean the wizards were trying to destroy *all* of the monsters?" A shocked expression covered Planter's face.

"Not all of the wizards were," Mapper said. "Just some. Other wizards tried to control the monsters, but it led to more violence and widespread destruction across many of the worlds connected to the Hall of Planes."

"You see?" Planter turned to Watcher and gave him an angry glare, her expression saying *you see, I'm right.* "Magic should be used *only* when needed."

"*Only* when *needed* . . . is that what you're saying?" She nodded.

"But when that giant creeper was charging and I told you to get to my side because I *needed* your magic, you didn't obey." Watcher frowned back at Planter. "What do you have to say about that?"

"Uh oh," Blaster said and stepped back.

"*Told* me . . . *obey?*" Now Planter looked furious.

"That might have been a strategic error," Blaster warned in a low voice.

The other villagers moved away from Planter.

"I didn't *obey* because I'm not required to *obey* you." Planter was furious. "Also, I didn't go to you when you *told* me because I hate using this magic, but you forced me to push that creeper away. It was going to blow you up because you just stood there, relying on your magic instead of using your head."

She turned away, toward the edge of the Lake of Fire. "I thought I knew who you were, Watcher . . . I guess I was wrong."

Watcher could hear her sniffling; she was probably crying.

"I don't mean to interrupt, but . . ." Fencer said in a meek voice.

"What?" Planter and Watcher asked in unison.

"Well, I can see a pathway down there in the lake." Fencer pointed into the water. "And also, there's no heat coming off these flames. I think they're fake."

Watcher stormed past Planter and stared where Fencer was pointing. Flames licked the surface of the lake, but she was right; there was no heat. Below the surface, an air-filled gap was clearly visible. It looked like a passage cutting through the water and extending into the deepest part of the lake.

"I say we just jump in there and see if it leads to Mirthrandos." Watcher glanced over his shoulder at the others.

"We aren't done talking, Watcher." Planter scowled.

"We're in a race with the wither king and his army of flying monsters," Watcher said. "It's important we keep moving. I hope you understand."

"Oh, I understand, all right." Her scowl turned into a frown.

We just have to keep moving, Watcher thought to himself.

"How do you know this isn't some kind of trap?" Blaster moved to his side and stared down at the submerged passage.

Watcher shrugged. "I don't, but there's only one way to find out. And if we don't find this great wizard, then we're stuck here with all these horrific monsters. I don't like that solution to our problem." He glanced one more time at Planter. Her face was still creased with anger.

"Maybe a trap down there will be a more merciful ending for you." Blaster laughed and patted his friend on the back.

"Possibly . . . let's find out." Watcher gave his friend a nervous smile, then jumped into the Lake of Fire, uncertain if he was jumping to his death.

CHAPTER 10

Watcher fell through the flames and splashed through a layer of water, then landed on his feet in a narrow passage. The fire had no heat and hadn't touched him, just as Fencer had suggested.

He peered up to the surface and found the flames were no longer visible; it was as if they had disappeared completely. Placing blocks under his feet, he raised himself up until his head was above the water. The other villagers gasped in shock when they saw him.

"Watcher, are you okay?" Blaster asked. "You don't seem to be dead. No burns?"

Watcher shook his head. "The flames are just an illusion. Jump in."

Without waiting for a response, he broke the dirt blocks under his feet with an iron shovel and descended back under the water.

Moving down the passage, he pulled out a torch and placed it on the ground. The flame cast a flickering glow over the passage, allowing him to see the soil under his feet and revealing sparkling bits of gemstones embedded in the blocks: diamonds, lapis lazuli, emeralds, and redstone chips glittering in the ground. Watcher looked at the walls and noticed there were none, just dark water reflecting the black sky overhead; the sun had not risen yet.

"I wonder what holds back the water?" Watcher reached out to touch the wall, but there was nothing there; his hand passed right into the cool water of the lake, but none of the liquid rushed into the strange corridor. "Some magic spell must be doing this."

Just then, someone splashed into the passage, and a moment later, Blaster appeared behind him, a surprised expression on his face. He moved along the narrow path with one hand sliding through the water.

"This is so cool." The boy smiled at Watcher, then moved farther down the trail, placing torches on the ground as he went.

More villagers splashed through the illusionary flames and fell into the passage, each with an expression of wonder on their face. Planter fell into the passage with her enchanted red shield ready in her hand. She glanced at the non-existent walls, then pushed past Watcher, not even glancing at him. He wanted to say something to her and somehow ease the tension between them, but he had no idea what to say. Instead, he sighed and waited for the rest of the party.

Mapper was the last villager to jump through into the Lake of Fire. The old villager looked excited when he splashed into the passage.

"That's not something I do every day," he said.

Watcher nodded, but said nothing.

"This is incredible. This wizard, Mirthrandos, must have used some kind of magical spell to keep the water from crashing into the passage and drowning us." Mapper reached out and ran his hand through the water. "I can't even feel the walls. I love this."

"Maybe we should get moving." Watcher's voice was filled with sadness. "If the wizard thinks we're attacking, he may turn off the walls, and then we *would* drown."

"Yes, of course." Mapper ran past.

Watcher followed behind the old man as the passage

sloped down into the depths of the lake. As they walked, the watery ceiling began to glow with reds and oranges as the sun rose in the east, painting the sky with its warm, colorful brush. From their viewpoint beneath the surface, the dawn colors seemed to mix with the water, shifting the lake above to a myriad of colors that grew darker as they descended deeper into the lake.

"This is beautiful," Mapper pointed to the color-changing ceiling. The old man stopped and just gazed up at the vibrant show.

Watcher gently placed a hand on his shoulder and pushed him forward. "We must keep moving, Mapper."

"I know."

As the sun continued to rise, the ceiling faded from dark blue to purple, then finally settled on sky blue, making the passage bright enough to remove their torches, using pickaxes to put out the burning sticks. The path moved deeper into the lake, toward their destination, which was now visible in the morning light: a huge airy bubble at the bottom of the lake, with an elegant structure sitting inside its dry hemisphere.

A large central building stood at the center of the bubble. Bright, blue-white sea lanterns dotted its huge, domed quartz ceiling, with splashes of blue-green blocks of prismarine creating elegant patterns, making the roof look like a beautiful work of art.

Smaller buildings connected by narrow corridors stood on the edges of the massive central structure. Blocks of dark-green prismarine marked the corners of the dwellings, with lighter blue-green blocks forming their walls and roofs. Sea lanterns, placed beneath windows and over doorways, spilled light across the structures, making them seem warm and inviting.

Watcher and Mapper reached the end of the passage, where the rest of the party was standing near the entrance to the structure. A large arched opening beckoned them to enter. It was lit with more of the glowing sea lanterns, the white cubes casting a pale blue glow on the surroundings.

"I guess we just go in?" Blaster asked.

"I don't know." Watcher shook his head. "What if we startle the wizard? We don't want him throwing balls of fire or bolts of lightning at us."

"Yeah . . . it might be dangerous." Blaster pulled out his curved knives. "You go first."

Watcher swallowed nervously. The opening to the massive structure seemed innocent enough; the arched entrance was large enough for six NPCs to walk in shoulder to shoulder. Two identical towers stood on either side, the cylindrical structures stretching all the way up to the top of the air bubble surrounding the compound. They were massive constructions, at least ten blocks across, with windows dotting their exterior, flickering light glowing within.

Watcher glanced up at one of the towers and thought he saw something move within. At the same time, the ground shook for a moment, as if struck by lightning, yet there was no flash of light or booming thunder, just a thudding vibration moving through the ground.

"Something about this makes me nervous." Watcher pulled out the Flail of Regrets and glanced down at it. *Baltheron, is this safe?* he thought to the weapon.

No answer came, but for some reason, Watcher thought he could sense the wizard smiling within the enchanted weapon. Frustrated, he put the Flail back into his inventory and took a step away from the entrance.

"Aren't you going in?" Planter asked. "You brought us here. You destroyed all those monsters up there, and now you want to leave?"

He remained silent, unsure what to do or say.

Planter frowned at him, frustrated. "You're all idiots."

With a scowl on her square face, she barged into the structure. Watcher glanced at Blaster, and the boy shrugged, then followed her.

"Let's go in." Watcher took out a wooden shield and followed, the rest of the villagers right behind him.

The huge entrance led to a large courtyard, the floor

checkered with dark and light blue-green cubes, each textured as if they were cobblestone, but with a blue-green tint. The walls boasted sections of quartz, too; the white cubes appeared harsh and bright next to the softer-hued prismarine floor. Countless bookcases stood along the edges of the wide courtyard, with tables and chairs distributed throughout. A large fireplace stood in the center of the room, with blocks of netherrack lining the bottom, but no flames filled the stone hearth; the fireplace was cold and lifeless.

At the center of the chamber stood an ancient-looking villager, their long gray hair hanging down to the middle of their back. An iridescent glow engulfed their entire body, with waves of purple light moving across their body as if it were alive. The wizard wore a long, flowing burgundy smock with gold stitching across the back and sides. Glittering bracelets adorned each wrist, giving off the same iridescent glow. The old NPC stood facing away from the newcomers, but Watcher suspected the wizard knew they were here.

"Are you the great wizard, Mirthrandos?" Watcher shouted, his voice bouncing off the blue-and-white walls.

The wizard stayed where they stood, their burgundy smock swayed back and forth as they shifted their weight from one foot to the other, the ornate gold stitching across the back glittering in the soft light from the sea lanterns.

Watcher moved closer, his whole body tense. "We're looking for Mirthrandos. We need his help to get home."

"You need *his* help, do you now?" The ancient NPC's voice was scratchy. It sounded old, like this building, like the Compass, like all the ancient structures built before the Great War.

"Yes, please. Is he here?" Watcher asked.

The aged villager chuckled, then turned around, and Watcher and the other NPCs gasped in surprise.

A woman, older than anyone Watcher had ever

known, stared at them, a huge smile on her wrinkled face. In her hands, she held a crooked wooden staff with bands of various metals wrapped around its length. Her body, bent with age, seemed frail and delicate, but her eyes twinkled bright green with vitality; they reminded Watcher of Planter's emerald eyes.

"I am who you seek," the old woman said.

"But I don't understand," Watcher said. "We're looking for the great wizard Mirthrandos. Where is he?"

Planter turned and punched him in the shoulder. "You're an idiot." She stepped forward and bowed. "Mirthrandos, it is a great honor to meet you. I'm Planter, and the knucklehead behind me is Watcher."

"You're *him* . . . um . . . I mean *her*?" Watcher stammered, realizing his mistake.

The ancient woman laughed. "You two are wizards?"

Planter shrugged, then nodded her head. Watcher moved to Planter's side and nodded, smiling, the purple glow from his arms casting a wide circle of iridescent light.

Mirthrandos brought her bright green eyes to Watcher and looked him over. When her eyes noticed the sparkling cape, they grew wide with surprise. "Ahh . . . Tharus' cape . . . you look like a real wizard, don't you?"

Watcher nodded proudly. It made the old woman chuckle, but for some reason, it felt to Watcher as if it were some kind of insult, as if she were mocking him.

"I hope you have better judgment than he did, young wizard." Mirthrandos' smile turned into a glare. She pointed at the rest of their company. "And the others?"

"Friends of ours," Planter said.

Some of the NPCs moved forward, revealing Er-Lan. Mirthrandos hissed and held out her staff, ready to attack, but Watcher jumped in front of her. Then the ground shook as if being pounded by meteors, and two huge iron golems stepped out of the quartz towers to stand in the arched entrance, stopping any hope of escape.

Planter instantly pulled out her shield, its edges wreathed in lavender flames.

Stepping forward, Watcher kept himself between the wizard and the zombie, his arms held out, showing he had no weapon. "That's Er-Lan . . . he's our friend." Watcher glanced nervously over his shoulder, then brought his blue eyes back to the old woman. "He is not a threat, and he's under our protection."

Planter nodded, then lowered her shield and stepped in front of Watcher. "We've come a long way to talk with you, and time is short. How about you put down that . . . whatever it is, so we can talk?"

Mirthrandos glanced at Watcher, then turned her gaze back to Planter and lowered her staff. "Well . . . you all seem harmless enough." She waved at the two golems, and the metal giants retreated back to their towers.

"Come closer, youngsters," the ancient wizard said.

"We aren't all kids," Mapper said with a smile.

"You are compared to me," she said. "I've been around since the Great War, so as far as I'm concerned, you're all youngsters."

Mapper's unibrow raised in surprise.

"As you know by now, I'm Mirthrandos." The wizard shot a glance at Watcher, then smiled knowingly. "And even though I'm not a *him*, I'm still the most powerful wizard alive."

Watcher felt his cheeks grow hot as he blushed. The other NPCs laughed.

"Now tell me, young wizard, why have you come to my underwater home and disturbed my boredom?"

Watcher took a step closer. "We need to get back to the Far Lands, and the Memory Stone told us you could help."

Mirthrandos nodded. Putting her wrinkled hand to her chin and leaning her banded staff against her chest, she stroked her long silver-gray hair.

"Rathenor is a big windbag. He likes to hear himself talk."

"Rathenor?" A confused expression spread across Watcher's face.

"Yes, Rathenor." Mirthrandos gazed at Watcher. "You must have figured it out by now . . . the wizards put themselves into key items to help with the Great War. Rathenor is the wizard who was transferred into the Memory Stone in case all of you came along."

"You mean there really was a wizard in that stone?" Mapper's eyes twinkled with excitement.

"Not his body, of course; just his mind and his powers."

"But . . . why?" Mapper asked.

"That's a story for another time. First, I want to know how you came to this land."

Watcher opened his mouth to speak, but Planter stepped forward first. She pulled the Amulet of Planes out from under her sparkling red armor. "We used this to get into the Hall of Planes." She pointed to Watcher. "We followed him here to stop the king of the withers from releasing his army from the Cave of Slumber."

"That didn't work out so well, did it?" Mirthrandos asked, fixing her penetrating gaze on Watcher.

The boy shook his head. "They got out somehow, and I'm sure they're headed to the Far Lands to destroy everything. We must get there first so we can form an army and mount a defense.

The ancient wizard smiled.

"What's so funny?" Cutter asked, his tone not exactly respectful.

Mirthrandos kept her eyes fixed on Watcher as the lavender glow around her body grew brighter. "This was how it started last time. Funny how history keeps repeating itself."

"Doesn't seem very funny to us," Watcher said with a scowl. "A lot of friends lost their lives trying to stop Krael and the Broken Eight."

"Wait—the Broken Eight?! They're here?" The ancient wizard actually seemed scared now.

"No. We destroyed them all," Watcher said.

"My Blaster destroyed the last one," Fencer said, her voice ringing with pride.

Blaster just rolled his eyes and moved a step away from her.

Watcher smiled, then turned back to the wizard. "We need to get portal keys so we can go home." He took a step toward the old woman. "We need your help . . . please."

Mirthrandos glanced around at the faces staring at her, her eyes darting from one villager to the next until they fell upon Watcher and Planter, who were standing side-by-side. "I had hoped we'd never need you two, but here we are."

"What?" Planter asked, confused.

"I don't understand," Watcher added.

Mirthrandos waved her hands, dismissing their questions. "I think it's time we visited the Weapons Vault. We'll find your portal keys there, as well as many other toys." She then seemed to get bigger as she stood up straight, her body no longer frail and bent with age. Now she appeared strong and vibrant, and the kindly, peaceful glimmer in her eyes was suddenly cold and dangerous.

The ancient wizard spoke in a clear voice that brimmed with strength and confidence, no longer sounding grandmotherly. "Everyone, follow me. We're going to Wizard City to unlock the Weapons Vault for the first time in three hundred years."

Before anyone could reply, she marched past them and stormed past the two quartz towers, heading to the stairway leading to the surface, the rest of the NPCs trying to keep up.

Watcher joined the rear of the group filing up the pathway leading out of the Lake of Fire, Blaster at his side. He glanced at his friend, an uneasy feeling in his heart. "She isn't telling us everything."

"I agree," Blaster whispered. "She's hiding some

secret, I could see it in her eyes . . . and I don't like secrets."

"Blaster . . . come on." Fencer stood at the foot of the path, one hand playing with the watery walls. When Blaster glanced at her, the girl's face lit up with joy.

Watcher chuckled.

"Don't start," the boy growled.

Watcher just smiled. "Payback can suck sometimes, and I think this payback is gonna suck for a loooong time."

Blaster punched him in the shoulder, his fist clanging off Watcher's diamond armor. With a resigned sigh, Blaster headed for the stairs, leaving Watcher behind.

As he headed for the stairs, he still felt uneasy. Something about this old woman just didn't sit right with him. Reaching into his inventory, Watcher pulled out the Flail of Regrets and held it up to his face.

"Baltheron, is there something I should know about Mirthrandos?"

But the presence within the enchanted weapon remained silent, amplifying his worries. With a sigh, he put away the flail and headed for the stairs, a feeling of dread creeping through his soul.

CHAPTER 11

A hot, dry breeze blew at the withers' backs as they floated parallel to the Creeper's Teeth, the constant east-to-west wind kicking up clouds of dust and making the lower-ranked withers, who were flying close to the ground, cough and wheeze.

The wither king looked up at the sun. Its harsh, square face had passed its zenith and was now beginning its slow descent to the western horizon. They had taken too long to get over the Creeper's Teeth, and that annoyed Krael.

The king of the withers glanced down at his army; many of the normally dark monsters were coated with a pale, grimy layer of dust. Some of them shook their shoulders as they flew, dislodging the fine debris, causing it to fall to the ground—or, more likely, to fall on the wither beneath them, but those above didn't care. Rank in a band of withers determined each individual's height in their formation, so the wither king flew well above the rest of his army with Kora at his side, avoiding the choking dirt. None dared fly higher, for that would be a challenge to Krael's command, which would have been an insult that could only be resolved through combat. No one would survive against Krael and his three Crowns of Skulls, and they all knew it.

"I can feel our enemy out there," Krael hissed, the center skull scowling at the distant horizon.

"How is that possible, husband?" Kora asked.

Center shook his skull, then glanced at Left and Right. They each nodded, confirming they also felt the boy-wizard's presence.

"The Crown of Skulls on each of our heads gives us this ability." A look of pride came across the wither king's face. "When we only had one Crown, the boy-wizard who calls himself Watcher eluded our senses. After I found the second Crown of Skulls, the boy's presence was like a tickle in the back of Left's skull."

"That's right . . . only *I* could feel the wizard's presence," Left boasted with a proud, scratchy voice.

"Shhh . . ." Right scolded.

Left scowled, but grew silent.

"Only after the last of the three Crowns was found could we clearly sense the pathetic wizard." Krael paused for a moment as Kora digested his words.

"The strange thing is, I can sense *more* of them now," Right said.

"Yes," Center nodded. "I felt it as well."

"Maybe someone chopped that boy-wizard in half," Left said with a smile.

"Left, behave." Center glared at the dark skull.

"Why do you think you sense more than one wizard?" Kora asked.

"I don't know," Krael shook his heads, uncertain.

"Maybe one of the foolish wizard's companions has magic powers as well," Right said.

"Then why didn't we sense them before?" Left's scratchy voice sounded like a challenge.

Right gave Left an angry glare.

"Perhaps their powers had not surfaced yet." Center nodded, then glanced at Kora. "The second wizard could have had his powers activated by something the boy-wizard used."

"Or maybe they found another magical artifact left over after the Great War." Kora moved closer to Krael. She lowered her voice. "Having another wizard to battle will frighten the others." She glanced down at the rest of the wither army, watching the shadowy creatures floating across the sandy terrain below.

One of the withers spotted a hideous creature on the slopes of the nearby Creeper's Teeth and fired a string of flaming skulls at the half-spider, half-zombie creature. The monster scurried back into its tunnel before the barrage struck.

"Krael, we need to keep this between the two of us until we know more," Kora whispered.

"Agreed." The king of the withers nodded, then closed all six eyes and concentrated on his enemies. The wizard and his friends were south of the wither army, but heading to the west, just like they were.

"Our prey moves in the same direction as us," Krael said in a loud, commanding voice. "We will find the Weapons Vault hidden in Wizard City, then destroy the fools that dare challenge us."

Many of the withers nodded their ashen heads eagerly.

"We still need to unravel the mystery of the riddle," Kora said. "Say it again, husband."

Krael slowed and turned, flying backward so he could face his shadowy horde. "The riddle goes like this: 'With feathers, I fly, yet I have no wings. My body is straight and true, and my head razor-sharp. I can be held in the palm of your hand, yet never thrown.' Every wither must think about this puzzle, so we can figure out what it means."

"I know what it means," a young wither said near the ground.

Krael glared at the monster, then motioned for it to approach. The little wither smiled, then floated upward, the other monsters scowling; this wither was likely the lowest in rank.

"What is your name?" Krael asked.

"I am Kobael," the tiny monster said in a meek voice.

"Tell me what you have learned about the riddle."

Kobael repeated the riddle. "'With feathers, I fly, yet I have no wings. My body is straight and true, and my head razor-sharp. I can be held in the palm of your hand, yet never thrown.'" The small wither glanced nervously up at Krael. "I figure the feathers are fletching. The body being straight means it's like a shaft, and the razor-sharp head is the pointy tip."

The little wither seemed proud of himself, smiling up at his king.

"So?" Krael demanded. "What does it mean?"

"Well . . . it's an arrow." The little wither smiled.

"An arrow?" Kora stared up at the sun, thinking to herself as the square, solar face slowly approached the western horizon.

"How does that help us?" Krael's left skull scowled at the small wither.

"Don't you remember?" Kobael asked. "You know . . . before the wizards finished the Cave of Slumber?"

Krael and Kora both stared down at the monster, confused.

Kobael stared up at Krael. "Just before they finished the Cave of Slumber, you led us, chasing a group of wizards across the land until they disappeared into the Valley of Arrows."

"What are you talking about?" Left asked, an angry and dangerous-looking expression on his dark face. "Are you making this up? Do you think we are fools? If we led such a battle, then we'd remember and—"

"I remember," Kora's center skull said, smiling to the tiny wither. "The wizards disappeared into the Valley of Arrows." She glanced at Krael. "You thought it was a trap, so we didn't follow, and rightfully so; with all the arrows shooting out of the thousands of dispensers, many withers would have died. Instead, we went around the valley and headed into the desert."

"That was when the wizards triggered the Cave of Slumber," Krael added.

Both Kora and Kobael nodded.

"That must be where the builder of the Hall of Planes, the wizard, Janus, hid the portal keys," Kora said.

"Then that is where we will go," Krael commanded. "Well done, Kobael. You will fly at the front of the formation, near us."

The little wither grinned with pride.

"But not quite this high," Left sneered. "Go down some."

Kobael's smile faded a bit as he descended.

"A little more . . . little more . . . there you go, right there." Left glared at the tiny monster.

Kobael stopped his descent and leveled off, still above most of the other withers. The little wither glanced over his shoulder at the other monsters. It brought a wide grin to his diminutive skulls again.

"Everyone, fly as fast as you can," Krael bellowed. "We're heading to the Valley of Arrows to find Wizard City." He glanced at Kobael. "You better hope you're right. If you're wrong and we're heading in the wrong direction, it may not go so well for you."

Kobael shuddered with worry, but held his skulls high and followed his king, the rest of the withers following close behind.

CHAPTER 12

The villagers followed Mirthrandos across the landscape, continuing westward. A wave of iridescent light flowed around the ancient wizard like some kind of ethereal serpent. It pulsed with power, casting a bright circle of lavender around her and completely overwhelming any light coming from Watcher and Planter; clearly, she was powerful. The purple glow mixed with the soft oranges and reds coming from the western horizon, where the setting sun was beginning its colorful show.

Worried about any more monstrous surprises coming from the leafy canopy overhead, Watcher put the company in a defensive formation as they ran. Fortunately, none of the treetop inhabitants tried to challenge them, though Watcher was able to see shapes moving across the leafy canopy; the monsters were still up there, watching and waiting.

The gigantic trees slowly grew smaller as they traveled through the biome, the forest gradually morphing into something Watcher would expect to see in the Far Lands: a birch forest with a smattering of oaks here and there and colorful splashes of flowers nestled within tall blades of grass.

The company darted through the beautiful forest, racing the sun as it slowly descended toward the western horizon. Watcher assumed they'd have to stop often so that Mirthrandos could rest, but the old woman had no problem keeping up with the rest of them. Her immortality apparently kept her fit as well. They ran in silence, each villager listening for the approach of monsters, but the forest was peaceful and calm. The sounds of cows, chickens, and pigs floated from between the pristine white birch trees, but as before, the animals were nowhere in sight.

"You notice it again?" Blaster said to Watcher.

"What?"

"Animal sounds, but no animals." Blaster pulled off his forest-green cap to scratch his head. His black curls instantly sprang outward, yearning for freedom, but were quickly captured again by the leather cap as he put it back on.

"Yeah . . . this is strange." Watcher pulled Needle from his inventory as he glanced to the left and right, looking for the animals, but finding none.

"Hey, Mirthrandos," Blaster said, moving closer to the old woman. "What was the deal with all the flames on the lake?"

"You liked my flames?" The ancient wizard smiled proudly.

"Well . . . not at first, but it was a neat trick."

"I put those there to keep anyone from bothering me in my underwater home." She glanced at Watcher and glared. "Apparently, it didn't work very well."

"You have to try much harder than that to keep Watcher from bugging you." Blaster laughed.

"Apparently so." She nodded, laughing with Blaster.

"Mirthrandos, can I ask you a question?" Planter swerved around a birch tree, then moved to the old woman's side.

"Of course, dear."

"You were around during the Great War?"

The old woman nodded. "Bad times, yes it was. Very bad times, indeed."

"How is it you're still alive?" Planter asked.

"I was given eternal life by one of our greatest wizards. Tharus was his name; that's his cloak your companion wears. I'm sure you've run across his name in books more than once."

Watcher shrugged, but Mapper moved to the young girl's side and nodded.

"I've read many accounts about Tharus and his incredible powers," Mapper said. "The books say he was powerful, wise and kind."

The ancient wizard laughed. "*One* of those three is true."

"You must have done something incredible to be given the gift of eternal life," Watcher said in wonder.

"Gift . . . ha!" Mirthrandos scowled. "It was a punishment."

"A punishment?" Watcher was confused.

The old woman nodded her head, her gray hair glowing a soft orange as the dusk sun spread its light across the landscape. "Yes, I did something that was unthinkable to the *great wizards.*"

"What did you do?" Planter asked.

Mira sighed. "I showed mercy to a monster." She glanced over her shoulder at the other NPCs. "All of you have learned to show mercy to a monster, even when you know what they are."

She pointed at Er-Lan with a crooked, wrinkled finger. "You know what he is, yet you allow him to be with your company, in peace."

"I don't know what you mean by 'what he is'. Er-Lan is a zombie and he's part of our family," Watcher said.

"Interesting . . . maybe you don't know." Mirthrandos smiled knowingly. "Back in my day, showing kindness to a monster was an unforgivable thing to do."

She reached out and put an arm around Watcher's glowing shoulders. "I showed mercy to a young wither who wanted no part in the violence spreading across the land. But when Tharus learned what I had done, he punished me by making me forever the caretaker of Wizard City and the guardian of the Weapons Vault."

"'Punished?' I don't understand." Watcher stared into the old woman's bright green eyes. "You can never die; how is that a punishment?"

"It is the cruelest and most severe of punishments. Tharus knew exactly what he was doing to me when he cast that spell." An expression of rage spread across Mirthrandos' wrinkled face. She steered around a thick copse of birch trees, then continued on their westward path. "He was cruelest of the wizards, though history paints him as a hero."

"I don't understand, Mirthrandos," Watcher said. "Not being able to die seems like a good thing."

"I've been alive for three hundred and seventy-eight years."

"Three hundred and seventy-eight?!" Watcher and Planter said in unison, shocked.

"Can you imagine how many husbands and children and grand-children I've had?"

"Well, I'd guess—"

"I've had to watch every one of them grow old as time ravaged their bodies. I've had to stand there, helpless, as they died in my arms, and had to grieve for them when their bodies finally disappeared from the surface of Minecraft." Her eyes glowed bright with anger and loss. "I've collected every bit of XP from each one when they passed so that I'd have something of theirs that would survive with me through eternity, but the one thing I didn't expect to survive all these years was the grief."

"That's terrible," Watcher said.

"It's so sad," Planter sniffled as a tear leaked from her eye. "That's why you know right where the Weapons Vault is located, right? You're its caretaker."

Mirthrandos nodded, her gray hair bobbing up and down.

"I'm sorry." Planter placed a hand on the ancient wizard's shoulder, but she brushed her hand away.

"I don't need your pity," Mirthrandos snapped. "I've lived longer than all you kids put together. I don't need anything from any of you. All I want to do is get you these portal keys so you can get out of my life and leave me in peace."

"But what about the war?" Watcher asked in disbelief. "Krael has been encouraging monsters to attack villagers all across this land. He has rekindled the Great War."

She stared at him with a blank expression on her wrinkled face.

"And now that the withers have escaped the Cave of Slumber and are free, they'll try to destroy everything," Planter said. "We need your help to stop them."

The wizard laughed. "My part in the Great War is over; Tharus saw to that. I see two wizards before me and others behind you who can help if you know where to look. This is *your* war now. My place is in my underwater home, staring at the squid and fish until time itself finally stops. That's what I have to look forward to; everything else is just a distraction."

An uneasy silence spread across the company as the woman's vile words, full of contempt at just being alive, etched their way into the NPCs' souls. Watcher knew everyone felt sorry for her, but that was no reason just to give up. He glanced at her and found Mirthrandos' eyes already focused on him, boring into his head as if she could read his mind.

Watcher was about to speak when the distant sounds of arrows zipping through the air filtered through the forest. Instantly, Watcher reached for the Flail of Regrets as Planter drew her red shield emblazoned with three wither heads across its red center, the rest of their companions grabbing their weapons.

"Well, look what we have here!" Mirthrandos stopped for a moment and knelt beside Watcher. She stared at the Flail, a huge smile on her face, then laughed. "It's like seeing old friends again. Hello, Baltheron, how are you doing in there?"

She smiled, then turned to Planter and leaned forward, as if speaking to the girl's shield. "Good to see you again, Sotaria; I didn't recognize you before." She laughed. "Is the tiny grain of your consciousness in there able to communicate, or did they divide you too many times?"

"What are you talking about?" Watcher asked.

"I knew your friends before they sent their minds into those weapons." Mirthrandos stared down at the Flail. "You've never looked better, Baltheron."

"You mean there really *is* a wizard in there?" Blaster asked in disbelief.

The old woman nodded.

"Huh . . . I thought he was just crazy when he was talking to that thing." Blaster smiled.

Watcher frowned. "Focus, everyone. We all heard those arrows just now. There must be skeletons nearby."

"Come . . . follow me." Mirthrandos moved ahead around a clump of bushes, allowing them to see the terrain ahead.

They pushed through the dense underbrush, the sounds of the arrows growing louder. Finally, then reached the edge of the tree line and stepped into a clearing. All of the NPCs gasped in surprise, Mirthrandos smiling. Before them stood a huge valley with a steep range of mountains extending out to the left and right on either side, making the edges of the valley impossible to pass. The setting sun cast a crimson hue across the landscape, causing long shadows to stretch out across the ground as if they were reaching toward the intrepid companions. Within the valley, tall columns of dispensers stood at least six blocks high, positioned all throughout the terrain, their faces pointing in every direction. Each dispenser spat out arrows, creating a constant storm of pointed shafts.

With the tall mountains to the sides, the only way forward was through the deadly valley.

"Welcome to the Valley of Arrows," Mirthrandos said. "This is the great secret of Tharus. Here lies the hidden Wizard City, and within it, the Weapons Vault."

"You mean we have to go *through* the valley to get to the Vault?" Mapper asked, his voice cracking with fear.

The ancient wizard laughed. "We don't go *through* the Valley of Arrows to get to Wizard City." She shook her head in disbelief. "The great Wizard City is *in* the Valley."

"But I don't see anything other than dispensers and arrows," Blaster said.

Watcher glanced around. There were a few steep hills of stone and gravel here and there leading to the Valley of Arrows, but no other features visible.

"Just follow me." Mirthrandos walked toward the edge of the Valley of Arrows, then stepped into it, heedless of the pointed shafts flashing through the air. In an instant, she disappeared from sight . . . and was gone.

"What happened?" Watcher asked, confused.

But before anyone could respond, a harsh laugh filled the air. Tiny square goosebumps formed on Watcher's arms as the cackle echoed around them.

"Krael," Blaster hissed. Watcher nodded.

The king of the withers, wearing three Crowns of Skulls, rose up from behind a line of trees, his army of dark monsters at his back.

"So, I see we meet again, boy," the wither king screeched.

Slowly spreading out across the treetops, each wither positioned themselves for a clear line of fire at the NPCs. The villagers cautiously backed up behind a nearby hill of gravel, terrified expressions on their square faces. Only Watcher and Planter held their ground.

"I think it's time for you to be deleted from Minecraft. First, we'll destroy your friends before your eyes, and then we'll destroy you." Krael laughed a cruel laugh. "Then, we'll begin the destruction of the Far Lands."

Watcher and Planter took a step backward, then another, both getting ready to turn and run, but then they saw Krael's eyes growing bright with rage. Seeing this, the other withers also prepared their own flaming skulls, their eyes getting brighter as well.

"Or maybe we'll just attack you first." The wither king grinned and glanced around at the members of his army. "Withers . . . FIRE!"

And hundreds of flaming skulls descended upon Watcher and Planter.

CHAPTER 13

A s the terrifying barrage of flaming skulls descended upon Watcher and Planter, they both shook with fear. Watcher knew this was the end; there was no way they'd survive this attack . . . it would take a miracle.

Suddenly, Planter raised her bright-red shield above her head. The metallic bands across the wooden rectangle glowed brighter with enchantments than he'd ever seen. Screaming her battle cry, Planter tensed every muscle, as if she were lifting a million blocks of iron; her voice was a razor-sharp knife, cutting through the roar of the fiery skulls, startling the withers.

Suddenly, lavender flames erupted from the bright-red shield and spread out, forming a magical sphere around Watcher and Planter. The flaming skulls crashed into the sparkling shield, each explosion a clap of thunder. The ground shook with every detonation, as did Watcher, but Planter held her sparkling shield with angry pride, refusing to back down. When the last of the skulls had exploded against the barrier, Planter lowered her shield and glared at Krael, a look of fury in her emerald-green eyes.

"That shield might protect you and the boy, but I

know you aren't powerful enough to protect all your friends." Krael turned to his army. "Move around that hill of gravel and blast them all!"

Before the withers could move, Planter screamed, "No! No! NOOOO!"

Her enchanted blue armor suddenly pulsed with sparkling red energy, and a blast of crimson light burst outward, causing Watcher to shield his eyes. The magical power sped toward the withers, lighting up the darkening forest before crashing into them like a mighty wave falling upon a fleet of boats. The radiant spell shoved the withers backward as if they weighed nothing, scattering the nightmarish army across the birch forest. They tumbled through the air like scattered leaves on an autumn day, their bodies smashing into tree limbs as they fought against the unrelenting tide.

"Quick, let's get back to the others." Planter turned and sprinted around the gravel hill with Watcher following close behind, still shocked at what he'd just witnessed.

When they made it around the hillside, they found their friends building defenses: fortified walls of cobblestones, archer towers, and large holes to hide in during the bombardments that were likely to come. With the sun now having set behind the distant horizon, the company of villagers found it difficult to see in the darkness, though the magical glow from Watcher's and Planter's bodies cast an iridescent light on their companions.

"I'm surprised to see you two still alive," Blaster said, grinning.

"Planter's shield bought us some time, as did her armor," Watcher said.

She scowled. "But we don't have much. The withers will be back, and I bet they're pretty angry now."

"You mean they weren't angry before?" Blaster asked, then laughed. He glanced at Watcher. "Any bright ideas?"

"Well . . ." Watcher glanced at the Valley of Arrows

behind them. Running through it seemed impossible; tall columns of dispenser blocks dotted the valley, their dark openings covering every possible route. Arrows zipped out of metallic cubes, their pointed shafts streaking through the air almost continuously.

"Here they come," Er-Lan moaned, pointing toward the forest as the wither king floated back up above the tree line, his face a visage of violent rage. The zombie backed away from the fortified wall and stood at the edge of the Valley of Arrows, deadly projectiles just zipping past his shoulders.

"Boy, it is time for you to watch your friends suffer," Krael screeched at Watcher in a fury. "The little girl's shield isn't going to help you this time, for now you must face flaming skulls from the king of the withers. And with all three Crowns of Skulls, my power is nearly limitless."

"Everyone back up." Watcher glanced over his shoulder. His companions were already standing at the edge of the Valley, as close to the dispensers as they dared without getting shot by the hundreds of arrows.

Ahead of them, Krael's eyes started to glow as did the three crowns on his skulls, as he gathered his power for another attack.

"Watcher," Er-Lan said, tugging at his sleeve.

"Not now." The young wizard was terrified.

"Watcher, Er-Lan thinks it is possible to go into the Valley of Arrows," the zombie said. "Mirthrandos went in; Er-Lan believes it is possible for others to follow."

"We'll never survive all those arrows," Blaster said.

Krael floated closer, getting ready to fire.

"No arrows," the zombie said.

"What?" Watcher asked, distracted.

"No arrows."

"What are you talking about?" Watcher glanced at the zombie. "We can see the arrows, and even hear them zipping through the air."

The zombie shrugged. "No arrows."

Krael floated high into the air with his eyes blazing. The three crowns gave off a bright iridescent glow, far more intense than any of them had ever seen, making many of the villagers shield their eyes.

"Now, it is time for you to die." Krael gave them a malicious grin, then launched his flaming skulls.

Suddenly, moving faster than Watcher had ever seen, Er-lan streaked in front of the NPCs with arms outstretched and barreled into his companions, shoving them backwards into the Valley of Arrows.

"Er-Lan, what are you doing?" Watcher shouted, trying to fight back, but for some reason the zombie felt incredibly strong.

The flaming skulls were almost on them now. Planter pulled out her shield as Watcher drew Needle, but before they could do anything, Er-Lan extended his scarred arms and pushed the rest of the villagers into the Valley of Arrows just as the flaming skulls struck. The last thing Watcher saw before falling backward into the Valley was the flaming skulls descending upon the spot where he had been standing.

As he fell, he closed his eyes, waiting for a hundred arrows to pierce his body. He was certain this was the end.

CHAPTER 14

L ying on the ground in the Valley of Arrows, Watcher held his breath, waiting for hundreds of arrows to pound into his diamond armor, reducing its strength until the crystalline coating shattered, leaving his flesh exposed.

But nothing hit him. The sound of the arrows was gone, as were the explosions from Krael's flaming skulls.

"Watcher, get up and look around." Blaster grabbed a shoulder and shook him. "We aren't dead!"

Watcher slowly opened his eyes and glanced around at his surroundings. All he saw at first was glittering purple and gold; his wizard's cape had landed on his head. Reaching up, he pulled the sparkling cloth down, revealing their surroundings.

The villagers were on the edge of a huge city entirely built from blocks of iron. Ornate towers stretched forty to fifty blocks into the air, their sides dotted with windows and balconies. Banners hung on the walls of the towers, each with different colors and designs, the long pieces of cloth fluttering in the breeze. Buildings of every shape and size covered the valley, with the smaller structures clustered around large palace-like constructions. Narrow bridges stretched from one tall structure to another, some piercing the walls of the soaring towers. The palaces and towers were stunning to behold, but paled in comparison to the structure at the center of the city.

There, a huge, elaborate creation stretched high into the air, dwarfing all the other buildings. It was shaped like a giant hand, and almost seemed to be reaching up into the sky, as if it were trying to grasp the sun. Watcher had no idea as to the height or size of the giant hand; it was too spectacular and colossal even to guess.

"Wow." That was the only thing Watcher could say, his mind reeling at the scale of the huge metropolis.

"What is this place?" Planter asked, stunned by the spectacle before her.

"This is Wizard City, of course," a voice said nearby. Mirthrandos stepped out of a complex arched doorway set into the side of a huge, octagonally-shaped building. The entire structure, like the rest of the buildings, was constructed completely out of iron. The ancient wizard reached out a wrinkled hand and rubbed the metallic wall as if she were caressing an old friend. A huge smile spread across her face. "I told all of you to follow me, but instead you stayed outside, playing with your wither friends. You need to be better listeners."

"The withers!" Watcher jumped to his feet and turned toward their attackers, remembering the danger.

Krael and his army were visible floating above the forest, though their images were distorted, as if being viewed through a stream of water. A huge cloud of debris floated in the air above a giant, newly excavated crater, the result of Krael's flaming skulls.

"As you have probably deduced, the Valley of Arrows is just an illusion I created to hide Wizard City," Mirthrandos said. "The magical shield will keep the withers from entering, but Krael's three Crowns of Skulls may give him enough power to penetrate the barrier. I suspect standing here is not such a good idea."

Watcher glanced at the withers again. The cloud of smoke and dust had now cleared, and a look of frustration was spreading across his three dark faces. The wither king was just realizing it: his prey had escaped. The monster tilted his three skulls back and screamed, each mouth gaping wide in rage, the sound of his wails blocked by the magical shield.

Krael glared at the barrier; Watcher felt sure the monster was looking straight at him. The monster's eyes brightened as the purple light from the Crowns grew intense again, and then he fired his flaming skulls at the barrier. The terrifying projectiles slammed into the enchanted shield with the strength of a giant's hammer. The magical shell over the city flickered for an instant, but held steady.

The wither king said something to the other withers, and in an instant, they were all firing their flaming skulls at the same location. A warm red glow formed at the point of impact, the energy from the assault slowly chipping away at the shield's strength. The monsters fired faster and faster, making the red glow ripple across the shield until, finally, the barrier ripped and collapsed. The terrifying screams of the withers, audible again, slashed through the air, driving icicles of fear into Watcher's soul.

The monsters stopped firing and approached the glowing hole, but it quickly healed, leaving the shield again intact.

"We need to get out of here," Blaster said.

"Everyone, follow me." Mirthrandos didn't wait. She spun and ran down a wide street, its sides lined with sparkling silver buildings. Putting her fingers to her mouth, the ancient wizard let out a loud, shrill whistle that was somehow amplified, making it echo across the city. Instantly, the sound of metal grinding against metal filled the air. It reminded Watcher of the Hall of Planes, and he quickly understood why.

Iron golems emerged from side streets and stepped into the avenue. The mechanical creatures looked almost the same as the guardians of the Hall, except for one feature: instead of a fist at the end of each arm, they had brooms or brushes or large blocks of wool attached to their wrists.

"What are they?" Watcher asked as he caught up to the ancient woman.

"They're the Keepers. All of the creatures in Wizard City play a role in the upkeep of the structures and buildings. These keep the streets and sides of the buildings clean."

Mirthrandos ran straight toward the mechanical giants, unafraid of their huge feet and stout arms. Behind the iron golems lumbered a group of dark golems made of obsidian, their black fists blunted like anvils. Following the golems ran about a hundred little metallic creatures, each the size of an NPC child or smaller, their metallic skins sparkling in the silvery light of the crescent moon as it rose in the east. Behind the tiny mechanical creatures charged a pack of shining metal wolves, their teeth razor-sharp. The mechanized animals howled at the moon as they charged toward the barrier at the edge of the city.

"My children," Mira said, her voice booming like thunder. "Protect the city. Drive the withers out."

The iron and obsidian golems lumbered toward the withers. The dark monsters were again attacking the shield, but this time, they hovered closer to their target. An orange glow formed on the shield as the flaming skulls hammered against the protective barrier. The shield flickered once, then tore, leaving a wide gap. The shadowy withers flooded into the city before the shield could re-form, angry wails coming from the monsters.

The golems moved toward the flying nightmares, but the monsters floated high overhead, out of reach. Suddenly, the legs on the iron golems extended, shooting their torsos into the air. The metal giants grabbed the withers with their tool-hands and pulled them to the ground. The dark monsters struggled in their iron grips, but could not escape. When they were within reach, the obsidian golems smashed their blunt anvil-like hands down upon the withers, crushing their HP and making the dark monsters flash red as they took damage.

More golems extended into the air, grabbing the nearest withers and dragging them to the ground. Howling their battle cries, the metallic wolves jumped into the air and bit at the withers' stubby spines as they struggled within the grasp of the iron arms, the wolves' sharp metal teeth taking more HP from the creatures. At the same time, the tiny, child-like creatures climbed up the bodies of the huge golems, then jumped onto the shoulders of the withers. Using knives and hammers connected to their wrists, the little mechanized creations smashed and stabbed at the withers, taking more HP. The rest of Krael's army tried to position themselves to attack the golems, but they couldn't fire without hitting their own.

"Withers . . . retreat!" Krael shouted, and the monsters fled Wizard City, floating up into the air and drifting out past the barrier, each glaring down at Mirthrandos and her legion of metal protectors. Krael abandoned those being attacked by obsidian golems, wolves, and metal children, allowing them to perish, their HP finally consumed.

The battle for Wizard City was over . . . for now.

"That was awesome!" Blaster exclaimed. "I loved it. Those golems—"

Er-Lan turned to the young boy and interrupted. "War should never be celebrated. All war is sad."

"Well . . . of course . . . I mean . . ."

"Er-Lan, what Blaster means is he's impressed with how well the golems can fight." Watcher placed a hand on the zombie's shoulder. "War is always the last resort."

"This zombie has learned it is the *first* solution for many, both zombie and NPC alike."

"Very true," Mapper said.

"Enough talk; those withers will be back . . . soon." Mirthrandos tapped her staff on the wall of a nearby building, the metal tip making the structure ring like a gong. The golems, wolves, and metallic children fell in behind her. "Come, we have much to discuss. Follow me."

Before anyone could speak, the old woman took off at a brisk pace, leaving the NPCs struggling to keep up.

CHAPTER 15

Krael's rage was a violent storm of shouts and flaming skulls, both directed at the protective barrier and pathetic inhabitants hiding underneath. The wither king glared at the illusion covering the city.

"I can't believe Wizard City was right there this whole time." He launched an attack at the shield, causing the illusion of arrows and dispensers to glow ever so slightly before fading away again.

Staring into the dark valley, Krael launched another stream of projectiles, each crashing against the defensive shell, leaving a faint glow at the point of impact to mark its boundary. Many of the withers fired their skulls as their king did, spraying the valley with their destructive projectiles. Krael knew the attack would have no permanent effect on the magical shield; he was just venting his anger. In order to break through again, they'd have to all fire at the same location, but those golems lingering about made it difficult.

"What were all those metal creatures?" Kora asked. "They destroyed many of our brothers and sisters."

"They're the caretakers of Wizard City," Krael growled. "The wizards called them the Keepers, and they weren't made for battle, but clearly they can fight."

"I've never seen an iron golem able to stretch up into the air like that," Kobael said, voice shaking. "They were terrifying."

"Be quiet, you tiny fool, I need to think." The wither king glared at the small wither. He hadn't seen Kobael in the fighting, but it had been chaos; maybe he had been behind Krael or out of sight behind a building. Still, the monster looked surprisingly unscathed.

"Husband, what is your plan?" Kora asked. "We can't let the boy-wizard reach the Weapons Vault before us. Those portal keys are critical."

"I know, wife, and I have a plan."

"Do you know where the Weapons Vault is hidden within Wizard City?" she asked.

"I have my suspicions," the wither king replied. "Their great wizard, Tharus, wrote about the Vault, saying no monster could ever reach it."

"Why is that?" Kora asked.

"The fool of a wizard said the defenses at the Vault's entrance were so strong, no host could ever overcome them. But he also said something else." Krael stared at the Valley of Arrows, the red glow below slowly fading away as the shield repaired itself.

"What did he say, husband?" Kora asked.

"Tharus said his Vault could reach up and touch the stars." Krael floated higher, moving over the top of the valley.

The silvery light of the moon shone down upon the withers, making each barely visible in the star-speckled night sky. They moved with their king, staying near, but, as always, none flying higher than Krael. From this height, Krael could just barely see a great iron hand at the center of the city peeking through the illusionary barrier of the Valley of Arrows.

"Do you see the tower at the center of the city?" Krael asked.

"You mean the large hand reaching upward?" Kora replied.

Krael nodded. "I bet those idiotic wizards put the Weapons Vault in the top of that tower, *'reaching up to touch the stars.'*" The wither king gave his wife a knowing smile.

"But if we mean to get into that tower, we'll need to find its entrance," Kora said softly, the other withers drawing nearer to hear better. "It will likely be heavily guarded by those iron and obsidian golems, not to mention the mechanical wolves and tiny creatures as well." She moved closer to her husband. "The entrance is probably underground, and you know withers are vulnerable when near the ground. Any attack at the tower's entrance would prove fatal for most of us."

The other withers nodded.

"We won't attack from underground; we'll fight the way withers are supposed to fight: from the air."

"But those iron golems—" a wither began, but it was instantly silenced by Krael's glare.

"The golems can't attack us if they don't know where we are." The wither king smiled maliciously. "We'll punch through their camouflage barrier, then spread out all across Wizard City. Our flaming skulls will fall upon them like a torrential rainstorm, hitting them everywhere, all at once; they won't know our real target until it's too late."

Krael slowly turned in the air, casting his gaze across his troops. Each had an excited and hungry expression on their shadowy faces.

"Listen, my brothers and sisters. Let me tell you how we will crush those fools in the City of Wizards and take the portal keys that rightly belong to us."

The withers nodded eagerly.

"We will remind the villagers why they should fear us. And when they beg for mercy, we'll destroy them, then head for the Far Lands to exact revenge for the past centuries of injustice."

The dark monsters shouted with excitement, some firing skulls into the air.

"Now come closer, my friends. Let me tell you the details of my plan."

As he explained, Krael's eyes filled with violent excitement, the three Crowns of Skulls glowing bright with magical power.

CHAPTER 16

Watcher followed Mirthrandos as the ancient wizard dashed through the maze of streets and alleyways, the tall iron buildings lining the streets around them sparkling with magical enchantments. The old wizard used the crooked wooden staff as a walking stick, its metal tip clicking against the ground with every step. The mechanical wolves and tiny metallic children, like miniature golems, ran next to the NPCs, their watchful eyes directed upward, ready for another wither attack.

"Mirthrandos, where are you leading us?" Planter asked.

"We need to find a safe place to talk and plan." She glanced over her shoulder at Watcher, shaking her head. "I didn't realize you were bringing a wither army with you. That changes what I had in mind."

"How?" Watcher asked.

"We'll discuss it when we get to where we're going." The old woman's voice was scratchy, worn down with age.

"And where's that?" Blaster asked.

"Here." The ancient wizard skidded to a sudden stop, the rest of the NPCs gathering around her.

Before them stood a massive building made, like all the rest in the city, from iron blocks. A huge arched entrance stood before them, its opening blocked with iron bars. Behind the metal barrier, blocks of nether-rack recessed into the walls burned with eternal flames, casting a flickering light on the interior. Watcher could see that chairs and tables covered the floor beyond the bars; he figured this had been some kind of meeting place hundreds of years ago. Now, a thick layer of dust covered everything, making the space look ancient.

Mirthrandos stood before the entrance and raised her hands high into the air. A purple light enveloped the woman's hands, the sparkling glow slithering from one arm to the next as she mumbled an enchantment. Then, a great flash of light burst from her outstretched palms, causing all the NPCs to shield their eyes. When the flash dissipated, the iron bars were gone.

"Come on in." Mirthrandos smiled at the surprised expressions on the NPCs' faces. "No one's been in this place for maybe two hundred years."

"It looks like it," Blaster said as he entered the struc-ture, his feet kicking up clouds of dust.

The ancient wizard scowled at the boy. "Follow me upstairs."

She walked to the right and ascended a staircase leading to the second floor, her staff tapping on each step. The NPCs followed the wizard up the stairs, accompanied by a dozen of the tiny iron children, with the mechanical wolves following close behind, the iron golems remaining out on the street, scanning the sky for threats.

Watcher climbed the steps behind Planter and Blaster with one of the tiny metal children at his side. He glanced down at the creature. Tiny iron blocks made up the creature's body, similar to the iron golems, but instead of having a bland, expressionless face, like the gigantic golems, this creature looked more like a young villager: Wide gray eyes glanced around nervously as it leaped from stair to stair. Long strands of silvery wire covered the metallic child's head, the shining strands bouncing about just like hair. The creature's mouth moved as if it were speaking to someone, but no words came out. It finally glanced up at Watcher, their eyes connecting. An expression of fear covered the creature's face as it quickly looked away, shaking in fright.

"It's alright, little one, I'm not gonna hurt you." Watcher put a hand on the little creature's shoulder. It flinched, as if expecting to be struck. "Don't worry, you're safe with me."

The metal child slowly stopped shaking and glanced up at Watcher again, then gave him a shy smile.

"There you go, it's alright. I'm Watcher." He held out a hand to the little creature.

The metallic child stared at the hand, not sure at first what to do, then stared at its own hands, where there was a brush connected to one wrist, a tiny hammer on the other. The creature disconnected the brush and put it into its inventory, then pulled out a hand and attached it to the empty wrist. It wiggled the fingers for a moment, as if checking to see if they were working properly, then smiling, the tiny creature extended its hand to Watcher. They shook, the little machine's posture slowly relaxing as the expression on its face changed from one of apprehension to happiness.

Finally, Watcher reached the top of the staircase and entered a large, dark room.

"Fixit, get the lights," Mirthrandos shouted.

"Fixit? Who's that?" Planter asked.

The little creature at Watcher's side made a squeaking sound and waved at her, then took off, speeding through the shadowy chamber. Redstone lanterns came to life as the mechanical creature dashed across the floor, flipping switches here and placing redstone torches there. In thirty seconds, a warm orange glow filled the room, pushing back the darkness, but not the chill. Watcher shivered, the others doing the same.

"Fixit . . . fire." Mirthrandos' voice was flat and without emotion; she spoke to the tiny metal child as if it were her slave.

Running to the center of the room, Fixit stood before a large firepit, where he removed the little hammer from his left hand and replaced it with a piece of steel. When he struck it with flint, the steel threw a shower of sparks onto blocks of netherrack within the pit, igniting the red cubes. The flames crackled as they burned off layers of dust, sending a gentle wave of heat throughout the chamber. Smoke billowed up from the burning blocks and flew up the chimney piercing the ceiling. As the warmth spread through the room, some of Watcher's stress eased. The villagers moved closer to the fire and sat in chairs surrounding the fireplace, holding their hands out to absorb the heat.

More of the tiny metallic children filed in the room and stood against one wall. The one who was apparently named Fixit stood in front of the other children, its silvery hair reflecting the orange glow of the fireplace and redstone lanterns, causing the long strands to shine with a warm, crimson luster.

Mirthrandos tapped her staff on the floor, making the iron under their feet vibrate. Everyone turned toward the sound.

"First of all, welcome to Wizard City." The ancient wizard stood before them, her long gray hair a jumbled mess after their sprint through the streets.

"Not a very nice welcome," Cutter growled. "You could have told us the arrow thing was just an illusion. We wouldn't have just stood there while the withers attacked."

"The Valley of Arrows disguise was common knowledge, or so I thought," Mirthrandos said.

"Maybe three hundred years ago, but today, that's new information for us." Cutter glared at the old woman.

"Huh . . . really?" The wizard didn't sound very concerned. "Well, I see you've met the mechites." Mirthrandos pointed to the metallic children.

"Are they alive?" Planter asked.

"Of course not. They're just metal contraptions I made a long time ago." Mirthrandos glanced at the tiny, metal creatures with a cold, emotionless expression on her wrinkled face.

Watcher glanced at the mechite standing in front of the others, the one he'd met earlier. "What about that one?" He pointed at the creature.

"Oh, that one. I named it Fixit. That's all it does. In fact, that's all any of them do: fix what needs fixing. They work with the iron golems to keep Wizard City in perfect condition. The mechites have no minds, no thoughts, and no ability to make decisions; they just fix what needs to be fixed." The old woman scowled at them as if the tiny metal children were insignificant bugs.

"They seem alive," Er-Lan said.

The zombie walked up to Fixit and ran his green fingers through the metallic creature's long, silvery hair. "Soft," the zombie said in a quiet voice.

Fixit smiled with pride.

"They look like they're alive to me, too," Watcher said.

"It doesn't matter what you think," Mirthrandos snapped. "They're tools to help keep Wizard City running, and they will be our guides to the Weapons Vault." The mention of the Vault brought everyone's attention back to the wizard. "Now, here's what I'm willing to do for you."

"Willing?" Blaster asked, eyebrows raised.

She ignored his comment and continued talking. "I'll take you to the Weapons Vault and give you all a portal key, and then you'll leave Wizard City and leave me alone."

"But we could use your help fighting the withers," Watcher said, taking a step toward the old woman. "The Great War is starting again, and we need your help to stop Krael and his army of monsters."

"Look, the wizards punished me for trying to help a wither who wanted peace. That punishment was . . ."

She paused for a minute, her eyes tearing up a bit as she thought about what eternal life had cost her. Then, wiping her face with a sleeve, she continued. "The wizards, in their vengeance, took every bit of empathy and emotion from me. I didn't care about their Great War centuries ago, and I don't care about your Great War now. I'm done being a good person and trying to do what's right."

She took a step toward Watcher, her hands glowing brighter.

"You're gonna take your portal keys and leave me alone; that's your only choice. If you don't like that, then you can leave right now, because as far as I'm concerned, the Great War ended a long time ago when the Cave of Slumber was activated. I'm not gonna help anyone or care about anyone. All I've gotten for helping others is pain and despair." The ancient wizard cast her gaze across the villagers, her eyes dull, as if there was no emotion left in her at all. "So that's the deal. Follow me to the Vault, or just go away; those are your choices."

Watcher glanced at Planter and sighed, then nodded. "Okay. Take us to the Vault, then we'll be on our way and leave you alone."

Without any response, the old woman moved to the nearest wall and pressed on some iron bricks. The block moved inward as if the entire thing were a button, the sound of metal grinding against metal filling the air. Nearby, the wall moved downward, revealing a dark passage. Torches flared to life, revealing a set of stairs descending out of sight.

"Follow me, and stay close if you want to live." Mirthrandos turned and dashed down the steps. Fixit and a dozen of the tiny mechites followed the woman, the metallic wolves trailing close behind.

"Come on, everyone," Planter said as she sprinted into the passage.

The rest of the NPCs ran into the passage, leaving Watcher and Blaster alone in the iron chamber.

"Something's wrong about all this," Watcher said quietly, his voice bouncing off the iron walls and returning as a ghostly echo. "Mirthrandos isn't telling us something."

"What do you mean?"

"Well . . . for starters, why are the withers here?" Watcher turned and faced Blaster. "And it seemed as if the golems were ready to defend wizard city, right where we battled the withers. Why didn't they come out of the city and help us?"

"I don't know. Maybe she really doesn't care about this war and the withers. Maybe she actually doesn't care about anything."

"Perhaps." Watcher nodded. "But that makes me trust her even less."

"Me too."

Watcher shook his head. "Come on, we should follow the others."

"Yeah, she did say 'stay close if you want to live.'" Blaster laughed. "Sounds like something I'd say."

Watcher chuckled. "True. Let's catch up with the others." He sprinted down the stairs, taking them two at a time as fingers of dread kneaded his soul.

CHAPTER 17

They followed the wizard and mechites through a series of twisting and turning tunnels. The passage descended deep into the bowels of Wizard City, with numerous side passages intersecting this one. At these intersections, Mirthrandos would sometimes turn and sometimes go straight. It was as if she were purposely trying to confuse Watcher and his friends, so they could never retrace their steps. And if that was her intent . . . it worked. The NPCs were completely lost and now dependent on the old wizard.

"This doesn't seem like a very direct route," Blaster said from the back of the line. "Where is this Vault anyway?"

"Did you see the main tower at the center of the city?" Mirthrandos's scratchy voice bounced off the walls of the passage, making it difficult to understand.

"Main tower?" Blaster spoke louder. "You mean the one that looked like a big hand?"

"That's the one," she replied.

"We're heading for the giant hand?" Watcher asked.

"That's what I just said . . . you don't listen very well, do you?"

"No, he doesn't." Planter laughed.

"Tharus had the mechites and golems build that tower. He cast the spells himself, making the walls more durable than just regular iron blocks. It would take a person with a diamond pickaxe years to dig through its walls. The only way in is through these tunnels."

"And a wither wouldn't want to go through these tunnels," Planter said, understanding.

The old woman nodded. "You're a smart girl."

Planter smiled.

"Oh, here we are: the Steps of Tharus." Mirthrandos stopped at a wide staircase made, of course, of iron.

The steps shimmered with magical power; Watcher could feel enchantments pulsing through the metal as if it were alive.

"These steps lead up to the Vault." The old wizard glanced over her shoulder. "Be quick or be left behind."

Then she dashed up the stairs, taking two at a time. The mechites moved with her, their little feet a silvery blur. A wave of shiny fur dashed past them all as the mechanical wolves sped up the steps, disappearing into the room at the top. Watcher sprinted up the steps after them, his shimmering cape fluttering in the air, the other NPCs followed behind. The villagers had trouble keeping up with the ancient wizard, but none wanted to find out what would happen if they were left behind.

When they reached the top of the staircase, the NPCs stopped and gazed in wonder at a huge, circular room, likely thirty to forty blocks across. It boasted an iron floor that had been polished to a mirror finish, leaving their reflected images standing directly below them. The shining surface was bright, as if lit with some internal fire, filling the room with silvery light. The chamber's ceiling was at least twenty blocks high, if not more, the iron roof dotted with redstone lanterns.

Colorful paintings decorated the walls; they were the most spectacular works of art Watcher had ever seen. These pictures were not the typical images seen in Minecraft, which were either portraits or pictures of skeletons, spiders, or other monsters. No, these pictures were something completely unique: each showed different battle scenes. One depicted the withers going into the Cave of Slumber; another picture was of a great host of monsters with the ancient zombie warriors called the Broken Eight at the head of the company; and the largest painting showing the construction of this tower. Each one was distinctive and filled with such incredible detail, Watcher suspected he could even see the faces of the characters if he moved close enough.

I'd bet these are images of battles from the Great War, Watcher thought.

You'd be right. A deep voice filled his mind; instantly, Watcher recognized it as Baltheron.

You've been unusually quiet, Watcher thought.

I've learned it is best to be silent when I have nothing to say.

We could have used your help outside of the city. Watcher's frustration grew. *You could have told us the Valley of Arrows was just an illusion.*

Baltheron remained silent within the Flail of Regrets. It made Watcher want to shout at him, but he knew it wouldn't do any good.

At the far wall, Mirthrandos stood surrounded by the pack of iron wolves, with the mechites motionless against the wall nearby.

"Come in," the ancient wizard said. "Don't just stand there at the end of the stairway gawking at the floor; your reflections won't bite, I promise."

The wizard laughed, then gestured for the NPCs to come closer. Slowly, Watcher moved across the floor but felt a moment of dizziness. With the mirrored reflection at their feet, the chamber seemed to extend downward, making the room's ceiling appear to be far below. The only thing to remind him he was actually walking on a solid surface was his own reflected image, which looked glued to his feet. Moving his eyes from the ground to the wizard, Watcher walked forward, ignoring his mind yelling at him that he was about to fall, and focusing instead on the hard floor under his feet.

Mirthrandos laughed again. "It takes people a little time to get used to that reflection. It was one of Tharus's many cruel jokes; he liked making people feel uncomfortable. For some reason, it pleased him."

Fixit scurried across the floor and grabbed Planter's hand with his left, then took Watcher's with his right. Other mechites followed Fixit's example, taking the hands of NPCs and helping them across the mirrored floor.

The group gathered around Mirthrandos. One of the wolves growled as Blaster took a step closer to the ancient wizard. Fixit moved to the metallic animal's side and stroked its fluffy, metal fur, calming the creature.

"Did you make the wolves, too, as well as the mechites?" Watcher asked.

"No, actually, I only made Fixit, and then he created the rest." The wizard smiled, pleased with herself.

Watcher glanced at the tiny mechite. The expression on Fixit's face was that of a proud father as he glanced across the chamber at the other mechanical creatures he'd created.

Suddenly, one of the wolves started to growl. At the same time, the muffled booms of distant explosions began to filter through the iron walls, sounding far away at first, but slowly getting closer. Mirthrandos moved to a wall and slid a block aside, revealing a hidden opening. She gazed across the city.

"Those foolish withers are trying to attack the city again." The wizard scowled. "It looks like they tore a hole through the shield somewhere far from here, and now they're attacking different parts of Wizard City at once." She glanced at one of the wolves, then nodded, and the animal took off running, a piercing howl coming from its mouth.

"The wolf will warn the golems." Mirthrandos smiled. "The withers won't bother us for long."

Watcher moved to the opening and peered out. Groups of iron and obsidian golems lumbered through the streets, pursuing the shadowy monsters. The withers floated all across the city, spread out from each other, likely so they could do the most damage possible, with many of them near the edge of the sparkling community. As the golems moved farther from the center of the city, and farther from the group in the tower, alarm bells started going off in the back of Watcher's mind.

"This is a trap," he said, suddenly realizing what was going on.

"What are you talking about?" the wizard said. "This tower cannot be entered other than through the tunnels. The withers would never try that."

Watcher moved to the center of the room. "Everyone, get out your bows." He turned to Planter. "I think we'll need your shield, too."

She looked at him, confused.

"Mirthrandos, where are the portal keys?" Watcher moved to the old woman's side.

"They're in those chests over there." She pointed to a far wall covered with wooden chests, each lid leaking a subtle purple glow. Running to a chest, Watcher flung open a lid. Inside were stacks and stacks of amulets just like the one Planter wore.

"Wait . . . leave those there!" Mirthrandos yelled.

"No, Krael is coming," Watcher said. "We need to hide them before he gets here."

"Watcher, what are you doing?" Planter asked, confused.

"I need you to trust me—all that is a trick." He pointed at the opening, where a group of distant withers was visible, their flaming skulls smashing down onto the structures below. "Just do what I say for once. We need your magic more than ever."

"You're going crazy," Planter shouted. "There aren't any withers here, it's just us, and you're being incredibly rude."

"I can feel Krael . . . he's near and he's come for the keys." Watcher moved to the next chest and lifted the lid. "Come over here, everyone, and start taking the portal keys."

"No, that cannot be allowed," Mirthrandos said.

"Watcher, you need to stop." Planter sounded angry. She walked across the room and yanked on his arm, causing him to drop a stack of amulets on the ground, the sparkling artifacts scattering across the floor. The red crystals at the center of the keys stared up at them, each glowing a violent red.

Suddenly, with a deafening boom, the entire tower shook, its walls and floor vibrating as if struck by a colossal fist. Another thunderous bang shook the tower, followed by another and another, until the ceiling started to glow an angry orange, then exploded. A shower of iron blocks fell to the floor. Instantly, the mechites moved forward to collect the debris and clean the area, their programmed conditioning causing them to move even though they all looked terrified.

Starlight sparkled through the hole, revealing the moon near the western horizon. Everything grew still for just a moment, the only sound being that of the mechites scurrying across the floor. But then, a wolf growled and looked up through the hole, followed by another and another, their eyes burning bright red and tails sticking straight out.

As the smoke and dust cleared, a vile, malicious laugh filled the air. "Hello, boy . . . we meet again."

"Krael," Watcher hissed, glancing up through the hole.

Krael hovered over the gash in the ceiling, three dozen withers floated nearby, each ready to fire their flaming skulls.

"I think you know what I've come for, and—" The wither king paused for a moment. "—oh look, Kora, they're spread out all across the floor, waiting for us."

Krael glared at Watcher, his eyes bright with hatred. "Withers, destroy them all . . . FIRE!"

CHAPTER 18

atcher sprinted back to the other NPCs, grabbing Planter's arm and dragging her with him.

"Planter, your shield . . . NOW!" Watcher shouted, as behind them the withers began to fire their flaming skulls.

Reaching into her inventory, Planter pulled out the magical shield and held it over her head, and instantly, bright purple flames sprang from the wooden rectangle, forming a wall of lavender fire. The flaming skulls smashed into the barrier and exploded, the heat from their blasts spreading through the chamber, but harming none of the villagers. On the other side of the room, some of the mechites were picking up the scattered amulets and tucking them into their inventories. Krael saw what the tiny mechanical creatures were doing and screamed in rage.

"Withers, stop them!" the wither king commanded.

Krael continued his attack on the villagers while the other monsters fired upon the mechites.

"No!" Watcher shouted.

He dashed across the chamber, drawing Needle in his right hand and holding a mundane wooden shield in his left.

"Watcher . . . look out!" Blaster shouted.

Watcher crouched behind his shield just as a flaming skull smashed into the wooden rectangle, shattering it into a million splinters. The noise from the blast was deafening, echoing off the walls and adding to the cacophony.

Another skull streaked toward him, but this time he was ready; Needle flashed through the air, striking the flaming skull and sending it back at its maker. The projectile struck the wither and exploded, making the creature flash red with damage.

Another skull was heading toward Watcher from a different wither, but he was already running. He sprinted to Fixit and scooped him up in his left arm. The tiny metal creature struggled to escape his grip, but Watcher held him tight.

"Mirthrandos, help us . . . fight back!" Watcher shouted, but the wizard just stood back against one wall, an expression of fear on her wrinkled face.

Watcher put away his sword and grabbed another mechite just as a second volley of flaming skulls headed toward him. Sprinting with all his speed, Watcher raced across the room and dove behind Planter and her shield just as the flaming skulls descended upon him. They smashed against the wall of purple flames, exploding with a blast of thunder, but leaving everyone unharmed.

Watcher set the mechites safely on the ground, then ducked as another attack smashed into Planter's shield.

"You doing okay?" he asked his girlfriend.

"What were you thinking! You could have been killed. Didn't you realize how dangerous that stunt was?"

"Sometimes I act before I think." Watcher shrugged.

"Really? I'm so surprised." Planter scowled.

More flaming skulls smashed into her shield, the blasts deafening.

"I had to save some of the mechites," he said. "I just couldn't stand there and let them be destroyed."

"You're being the weapon again, acting as if you had

no choice." Planter's voice resonated with anger. "You could have said something and all of us could have helped."

Watcher shrugged just as more flaming skulls exploded, filling the iron chamber with heat and noise.

"I guess. How are you holding up?"

Planter shook her head. "I'm getting tired."

"Hold on a little longer."

Just then, a barrage of flaming skulls fell upon the remaining mechites, enveloping them in the lethal flame. The explosion made all of the tiny creatures flash red just once, then disappear, leaving behind glowing balls of XP.

Fixit screeched in despair and fell to the ground. Tiny metallic tears flowed from the mechite's eyes as the little mechanized creature wept.

The withers swooped down where the ill-fated mechites had been standing and retrieved the portal keys. Wolves dashed forward and leapt into the air, their sharp teeth seeking wither bones, but the dark monsters blasted the metallic animals, burning away their HP until no more remained.

Then, one of the withers moved to the chests and smashed one, then another, causing more of the portal keys to spill across the floor. The monsters moved across the shining floor, allowing the amulets to move into their inventories, then floated high into the air again, out of reach.

Watcher screamed in rage as Krael renewed his attacks on Planter and her shield. The flaming skulls, energized by the Crowns of Skulls, were taking their toll; Planter's shield was showing little cracks across the back as the projectiles continued to hammer against it.

"Planter, we have to stop Krael." He put a hand in the center of her back. "Move forward."

Watcher dropped Needle and pulled out the Flail of Regrets. He pushed Planter forward, stepping toward Krael.

"No . . . I can't," Planter moaned. "My power is draining."

"Just hold on to that shield," Watcher said. It was more a command than a request.

He swung the Flail of Regrets over his head, gathering momentum as they neared the king of the withers. Krael's eyes grew bright as they neared, his fireballs growing even stronger as he drew upon the magic in the crowns.

"Keep going," Watcher ordered.

"I can't . . . I can't."

"We have to stop him," Watcher said. "We're the only wizards that can do it."

"Listen . . . I can't do it."

"Yes you can!" Watcher pushed her forward another step, his left hand at the center of her back.

Then, swinging the Flail with all his strength, Watcher attacked the wither king, the spiked ball extending forward, trying to reach the floating creature. But just before it hit him, Krael rose abruptly into the air, allowing the spiked ball to pass underneath.

"Come, my brothers and sisters," the wither king shouted. "We have what we wanted. Now it's time to celebrate with the destruction of the Far Lands."

The withers laughed, then floated out of the tower. Planter finally dropped her shield and collapsed to the ground, exhausted. Moving to the center of the chamber, Watcher stared through the hole in the ceiling, watching the blanket of stars slowly dimming as the sun rose in the east. The withers floated around the outstretched fingers atop the tower, then flew away, disappearing from sight.

"They have the portal keys," Watcher said. "The Far Lands and all our friends and families are lost."

CHAPTER 19

Watcher walked across the floor and looked down; the portal keys that had been lying there were now gone, taken by the withers. Multiple chests lay on the ground, their lids either flung open or broken off, the wooden boxes now empty.

"The withers have the amulets." Despair spread through Watcher like a fever. "Now Krael and his army can get to the Far Lands and destroy everything. What are we gonna do?"

"Watcher," Blaster said, but the young wizard ignored him at first. "Watcher! Get over here . . . it's Planter."

He spun around. Blaster was kneeling on the ground next to Planter's collapsed form, her bright-red shield with the three black skulls emblazoned across the front resting across her armored chest. The glow from the shield matched the iridescent light coming from the girl's arms, but now it seemed even brighter.

Watcher sprinted across the room and knelt by her side.

"Planter . . . are you okay?"

Her head moved from Blaster to Watcher, her eyes clouded with confusion. Pulling a splash potion from his inventory, Watcher smashed it across her glittering, blue chest plate. The liquid instantly soaked into her flesh, adding to her health, but she still looked confused.

"What's wrong?" Watcher sat her up and wrapped his arms around her. "Planter, you'll be alright in just a minute."

He glanced toward Mirthrandos who was on the far side of the room, seemingly unconcerned.

"Mirthrandos, help her," Watcher pleaded.

"She's fine," the ancient wizard said. "The girl just needs to come to terms with her power. I bet she was able to use magical items in the past because she was a descendant of a wizard, probably from Sotaria, the maker of that shield. But now, using the shield has unlocked more of her powers."

Mirthrandos pointed at Planter. "Look at how bright her arms and chest are now." Watcher glanced down. Planter's upper body glowed like his and the old woman's, or maybe even brighter; the iridescent light moved across her like a living organism, pulsing with each heartbeat.

The ancient wizard moved closer and stared down at the confused girl.

"You're a wizard, Planter." Mirthrandos smiled. "Get used to it."

"Nooooo," Planter moaned. "My mother always warned me about this. There was a curse in our family, and this was it." She glanced up at Watcher. "My mom told me to stay away from enchanted items and witches with their potions, and anything involving magic." Her eyes narrowed as they filled with anger. "But you had to push me to use that shield."

"We had no choice, Planter. The withers would have killed us all. You saved everyone."

Planter stared at the other side of the room, where balls of XP lay scattered across the ground like discarded pieces of trash. "I didn't save *them*, did I?"

"They were just mechites . . . who cares about them?" The old woman walked over and collected all the XP. "They are just mechanisms, not living creatures. They don't think or feel or—"

Suddenly a loud squeal cut through the room. Fixit glared furiously at the ancient wizard, then scurried to Planter's side and looked at her as a tiny metal tear fell from the creature's eye. Reaching down, Fixit removed the hammer attached to his right wrist and replaced it with a metallic hand, then raised the hand over his head, fingers spread wide.

Planter nodded and stood, then raised her own hand up into the air. She glanced at Watcher and Blaster. The two boys understood and did the same, giving the Salute to the Dead for the fallen mechites.

"What are you doing? They're just machines," Mirthrandos objected. "I built Fixit, who built them."

"Then I think you did your job too well," Watcher said. "If they have XP, then they have souls."

Keeping his hand up and his fingers spread wide, he glanced at the other NPCs, who all had their hands raised in the air too. The few surviving iron wolves howled, their majestic voices filled with sorrow. Watcher squeezed his hand into a fist, then lowered his arm. Next to him, Watcher could hear Fixit's hand creak and groan as metal bent within the mechite's fist. When the tiny little creature lowered his arm and opened his hand, Watcher saw that, in Fixit's grief, he'd squeezed too hard, and the metallic fingers had dented his palm, damaging it.

Watcher knelt next to Fixit, put an arm around his diminutive shoulders, and hugged him. "We'll stop Krael somehow and make sure these withers never do anything like that again."

Fixit looked up at Watcher, and a strange crooked smile spread across the mechite's face. Then the creature gave off a purring sort of sound that eased some of Watcher's fears. He knew this little mechanical being had faith in him, but did anyone else?

Glancing at Planter, he adjusted his cape so it hung straight down across his back, then raised one side of his unibrow in an unasked question. "Well, Planter?"

She shook her head, an uncertain expression on her face.

"Planter, I need your magic to stop Krael. I need your shield. I can't do it alone."

Her face changed from one of uncertainty to anger. "You need my *magic*?"

Watcher nodded.

"You need my *shield*?"

He nodded again.

"What about *me*?"

"I don't understand," Watcher said.

"Do you need me?" she asked.

"Well . . . umm . . . of course I do," Watcher replied.

Planter grew even angrier, her unibrow creased with frustrated rage. "My parents were right. All you care about is my magic, not me!"

"No, that's not—"

"I hate magic. It ruins everything." She balled her hands into fists and glared at Watcher. "And now, magic has even made me hate you." She threw her shield to the ground, then turned and headed for the exit and sat down on the iron steps. "I'm done with you, and I'm done with your war . . . it's over."

"But . . ." Watcher didn't know what to say.

The other NPCs turned and followed her, some of them sitting down on the steps as well, looks of defeat on their faces. They all knew what would happen when the withers went through the portal; it would mean the end of the Far Lands and all their families. But they also knew what would happen to them if they tried to stop the dark army: they'd all perish.

Watcher looked at Blaster, hoping for some support.

"The withers have the portal keys. There's no way to stop them now." Blaster lowered his head, an expression of defeat on his square face. "Like Planter said, it's over . . . we lost."

The boy moved to the stairs and sat next to Planter. She leaned into Blaster and rested her head on his shoulder, eyes cast to the ground. Everything around Watcher felt dark and cold, the bitter taste of defeat filling his soul.

"But what about my father and sister?" Watcher said softly. "They'll be . . ."

He couldn't finish the sentence as he imagined what the withers were going to do to the Far Lands. He saw smoke billowing into the air, forests turned to ash, villages flattened to the ground. It would be total devastation, and all because he had failed.

With the last bit of hope evaporating from his soul, Watcher sat on the ground and hung his head, despair enveloping his soul. *What am I gonna do . . . what am I gonna do?* he thought, but no answer came, because none remained within him—just grief for what would soon be happening to everyone he'd ever known.

CHAPTER 20

Watcher felt darkness spread across his soul, the emptiness within him filled with grief and despair; it was as if a heavy black shroud had settled over him. Closing his eyes, he could imagine the terror his father and sister would experience when the army of withers came knocking on their door.

I failed you, Dad and Winger, he thought, the words like poison, eating away at his mind.

Tears welled up in the corners of his eyes, but he refused to set them free. Images of his sister being blasted by Krael's flaming skulls nearly released the tiny cubes of moisture from his eyes; Watcher just barely retained control.

I don't want to cry . . . I don't want to cry. The thoughts felt hollow in his pathetic excuse for a brain. *I failed them, and now they'll be destroyed because of me.*

He pulled out one of the portal keys from his inventory and stared down at it. The shiny metal artifact looked identical to the Amulet of Planes that Planter had found in the Wizard's Tower so many weeks ago.

That's because it is *the same,* an angry voice said in his mind.

Watcher sat up and glanced around. No one was

nearby; all of the NPCs were now sitting on the steps leading out of the chamber, the morning sunlight streaming in through the massive hole in the ceiling, falling upon their slumping forms. Where the sun's rays fell upon Planter's beautiful blond hair, it shimmered like spun gold.

Was that you, Baltheron? Watcher asked.

Of course it was me. Were you expecting someone else? the artifact said.

Watcher reached into his inventory, pulled out the Flail of Regrets, and set it on the ground, then put his enchanted sword Needle next to it.

Why did you put your . . . mind, I guess, into this weapon?

We did what was necessary to counter the living weapons being made by the monsters, Baltheron said. *This was the only way to win the war: by sacrificing our magic and XP and minds. These weapons, when in the hands of true warriors, turned the tide and saved Minecraft from destruction.*

But why make the wielder feel such pain? Watcher asked. *The first time I used you, my health was torn out of my body; it was terrible.*

It was to make sure I knew who you were. If you had been a monster, I would have destroyed you. By sampling your health over and over, I realized you were the one we were looking for: a descendant of the wizards.

So . . . who is in the other weapons?

I'm Dalgaroth, Needle said, the wizard's voice high-pitched.

And I'm Taerian, the Gauntlets of Life reported, the magical artifacts on Watcher's wrists pulsing with iridescent energy. *We were some of the strongest wizards, and were sent to fight the withers in the Great War, but now they're free.*

I know, Watcher said. *I failed.*

Quit feeling sorry for yourself, Baltheron said, his tone angry and abrasive.

What do you mean? Watcher thought. *We're defeated. I have every right to feel sorry for myself.*

No, you don't! Dalgaroth shouted, his voice now even more shrill. *You're a wizard, and that means you have a responsibility to protect everyone, whether you like it or not.*

Dal is right, Taerian said. Watcher's wrists felt warm when the Gauntlets of Life spoke in his mind. *When we thought we were going to lose the Great War, we didn't just sit down and give up. We came up with a plan.*

And that's when we created all of these weapons, Baltheron added, his deep voice calming. *We realized the courage and determination of the warriors using these weapons were more important than just some wizards with magic. It was the villagers' hearts that made the difference during the Great War, and they'll make the difference now.*

Wait . . . you said 'all these weapons.' What weapons? Watcher stood, staring down at Needle and the Flail. *I have a couple and Planter has a shield. That's hardly enough for all of the villagers here. And even if it were, there are less than twenty of us and hundreds of withers. How can we stand up against those odds?*

The three weapons all chuckled, as if they knew a secret.

We faced a similar situation. But then we realized magic weapons could make one person as strong as five monsters.

"Five?" Watcher said aloud. Some of the NPCs raised their heads and glanced in his direction.

Are some of them ranged weapons? Watcher stared at the Flail of Regrets. *You know, like bows and arrows.*

The three ancient wizards laughed again.

You have no idea, Baltheron said. *Break the bottom chest against the far wall.*

Watcher stood and walked to the opposite wall. He could feel the eyes of his friends on his back, but none stood to ask what he was doing or offer to help. Putting the weapons back into his inventory, Watcher pulled an ax from his inventory and smashed it into the bottom chest.

"Watcher, what are you doing?!" There was an angry tone to Planter's voice.

"I'm not sure destroying things is gonna help," Blaster said sadly.

"Leave him be," Mirthrandos said, her whispering voice barely audible over Watcher's chopping at the chest. "They won't help him."

"What do you mean, 'they?'" Blaster asked. "What's going on?"

"Maybe if you had a hundred wizards." Mirthrandos stared down at Blaster, then cast her eyes across the group of NPCs. "All you have here are villagers with no magic, and without any special powers; it's hopeless. You're better off finding a place to hide and staying there for the rest of your life rather than trying to stand up against the withers."

Watcher heard the old woman's words, but ignored her, focusing instead on his task. He smashed the chest with his axe again and again until it finally shattered, throwing more of the portal keys across the ground.

Dropping his axe, Watcher knelt and pushed aside the shimmering amulets, revealing a secret chest recessed into the floor. Using both hands, he carefully lifted the lid, the hinges creaking their complaints about the centuries of neglect. Watcher gasped when he saw the contents.

"What is it?" Blaster ran to Watcher's side. He too gasped in surprise.

Inside the chest was row upon row of enchanted bows, each shimmering with magical energy.

Break the other chests and look underneath, Baltheron said, his deep voice sounding pleased. *These are the tools you'll need to make your stand.*

Watcher picked up his iron axe and smashed the next chest; more portal keys flew across the floor when it shattered, revealing another sunken chest filled with magical weapons. He broke the next chest and the next chest and the next until he'd revealed all the hidden containers, each filled with different tools of war.

The other NPCs now approached, each curious about the chests' contents. Watcher reached into one, then emerged with two long, curved swords, each the length of his arm, the weapons sparkling with magical power. The villagers gasped in surprise, then rushed to his side and gazed at the enchanted weapons.

These weapons each contain a small piece of a wizard's mind, Taerian said, his voice scratchy and rapid, the words shot out like staccato drumbeats. *But they will not harm the wielder; we have told the slivers of consciousness in each that you are all friends. Be warned, though: these are powerful weapons, and should be used with care.*

Watcher tossed the two curved blades back into the chest, then glanced at his friends.

"We can still defeat the withers. The element of surprise will be on our side, and the magic in these weapons will even the odds." Watcher pulled Needle from his inventory and tapped it on the ground, making the iron floor ring like a bell. "I know this is terrifying, and you're all afraid. But I'm telling you . . . we can do this."

He moved toward Planter, but saw her tense up, making him stop. "Planter, everything you said to me was right. I was thinking about your magic more than I was you. But I'm so scared for my family and everyone in the Far Lands. You're right, people are more important than things. But our friends and families won't be enough to stop the withers without our help."

He turned to look at the other NPCs, most of whom were still standing near the chests of magical weapons. "The people necessary to stop the withers stand before me, and now we also have the tools to make it possible."

He moved to one of the chests and pulled out a sparkling bow. Turning to a vacant wall, he pulled back the bowstring; instantly, a sparkling arrow appeared on the string. When he released it, five arrows sprung from the bow and streaked across the chamber, each shaft trailing a line of glowing iridescent particles. The arrows struck the iron wall, making the chamber ring like a huge gong. Watcher smiled, then turned back to glance at his friends.

Just then, the bow in his hands dissolved into dust. *Some of these weapons last for only a short amount of time, so use them with care, for they will only be useful for a few minutes,* Baltheron said.

"Apparently, many of these weapons won't last long, but I think they will serve us well." Watcher kicked at the pile of dust with his diamond-clad foot, then looked at his friends.

"I refuse to give up. I refuse to let Krael and his horde destroy the Far Lands. Our family and friends are counting on us, and I'm not gonna let them down." Watcher reached up to his shoulders and yanked off the sparkling cape, the symbol of his importance as a wizard, and then threw it to the ground.

"I don't care what anyone thinks about me. I don't care if they know I'm a wizard or not. All I care about is the people who need my protection." He kicked the cape across the floor, the shimmering gleam from the rich fabric slowly fading from sight.

"I refuse to give up." He glanced at Planter, a serious expression on his square face. "It's time for action."

The NPCs remained silent, some of them glancing at Planter, whose brow was furled with anger.

"You can't just take on an entire army of withers." She stood and planted her fists on her hips, glaring at Watcher.

"Yes, I can." He focused his gaze on her, his blue eyes fixed to her emerald greens. "And I will, even if no one will help me." He took a step closer to her. "I refuse to give up."

"Magic will only bring trouble. My parents were right about it, and now look at us." Planter glanced at the other NPCs, her eyes filled with a cold rage. "Magic doesn't care about us."

Then Planter pointed at Mirthrandos. "She doesn't care about us. If we take up these enchanted weapons and stand up to the withers, it'll be to our ruin."

Some of the NPCs nodded their heads, clearly in agreement.

Watcher took another step toward her and softened his voice. "I'm tired of being pushed around by Krael. He and his horde of monsters are like every bully who ever picked on me back home. The wither king isn't gonna stop with just the destruction of the Far Lands; he'll try to destroy all of Minecraft."

He turned and faced the other NPCs. "All my life, I wanted to be someone important . . . you all know that. I had that disastrous attempt at joining the army, and it failed. When the zombie warlord came to our village and destroyed everything, those monsters thought I was so pathetic, I wasn't even worth being taken as a prisoner. When we chased the spider warlord, I led our company into countless traps; who knows how many villagers were killed because of me?"

He turned back to Planter, a tear in the corner of his eye. "I'm tired of being a failure, and I'm tired of pretending to be something I'm not." He reached a hand out to her, but she stepped back, looking away. "You were right when you questioned whether I was the weapon or the wielder. The weapon has no choice but to act out of violence, but the wielder can choose to fight or not."

He glanced at the other NPCs, then stepped forward and stamped his foot down upon the wizard's cloak. Rage filled every fiber of his being, causing his voice to growl like thunder. "Right now, I choose to be both the weapon and the wielder. I am Watcher, son of Cleric, the smallest and weakest NPC ever to walk the Far Lands, and I refuse to give up."

He glared at Mirthrandos. "It's time we taught the

withers why they should be afraid of NPCs. I'll do it alone if I must, but it *will* be done."

"Not without me." Blaster reached into a chest and pulled out two more curved, enchanted swords. He swung the blades around his body in a flourish, their keen edges leaving a trail of sparks as the magical weapons sliced through the air. "Now *that's* what I call a knife."

The other NPCs stood there, an uneasy silence draped across the chamber as Planter and Watcher stared at each other, a silent contest of wills underway.

Just then, Fencer stepped forward and grabbed a curved sword. Looking down at it, she smiled, then jumped into the air, swinging the blade with lightning speed as she did a flip, shocking them all. When she landed on the ground, Fencer brought the magical blade down upon one of the wooden chests, shattering the lid and spilling countless enchanted bows upon the ground.

"Nice." Blaster nodded, eyes wide with surprise.

She smiled at him, then scooped up multiple bows and stuffed them into her inventory.

Mapper gave Watcher a wink, stepped forward and took a handful of bows, and then also grabbed a long, dangerous-looking spear, its metallic point razor-sharp and shimmering with magic. He pounded the end of the spear on the metallic floor, making the chamber ring. More NPCs stepped forward, grabbing swords and spears and tridents and battle axes, each weapon sparkling with power.

"You can't do this!" Mirthrandos shouted over the commotion. "You can't just go fight the wither army. There are too many of them! You'll all be destroyed."

"We won't abandon our friends." Watcher glared at her, then turned his gaze to Planter. "We need you too."

Planter glanced at the other villagers, then sighed. "All right."

She looked Watcher straight in the eyes. "Since you're forcing me to do this, and all you care about is my magic . . . you can have it. But that's all you'll ever get from me; the rest—" she said, putting her hand over her heart, "—is gone. You and me . . . we're done. I can't trust you when all you care about is magic and power."

Moving to the chests, Planter grabbed a handful of bows and stuffed them into her inventory, then stepped back, not meeting Watcher's eyes. As the other NPCs finished gathering weapons and various potions stored in some of the chests, Fixit gave off a squeak, then tapped his tiny foot on the ground. The other surviving mechites turned to their leader, confused expressions on their shining faces. Fixit glanced up at Mirthrandos, then pointed to Watcher, as if demanding something from the woman.

"No . . . I won't help," the ancient wizard said. "Even though I don't age anymore, that doesn't mean I can't be killed. Those villagers are going off to their death, and I won't be a party to it."

Fixit stamped his foot on the ground in frustration.

"I said no!" Her voice boomed through the chamber, magically amplified.

The other mechites cowered in fear, all except Fixit. The tiny creature stood tall, glaring up at the old woman. She just shook her head, then turned away.

Fixit stamped his foot again, then walked toward the chests of weapons. Reaching down, he picked up one of the bows and held it over his head, the weapon looking gigantic in his little hands. The other mechites saw the gesture and jumped up and down, squeaking with excitement.

"I said NO!" Mirthrandos pointed her crooked staff at Fixit. Suddenly, an iridescent glow wrapped around him, causing the tiny creature to freeze in place. He dropped the bow, the enchanted weapon clattering to the ground.

"What are you doing?!" Planter shouted.

Before she could move toward Fixit to help, the shell of purple light dragged him across the ground and back to Mirthrandos' side.

The wizard glanced down at Fixit. "I said no, and I mean it."

The glowing envelope of light faded away, leaving Fixit standing there, shaking in fright.

"You better not have hurt him," Planter hissed.

Watcher stepped forward, the Flail of Regrets and Needle in his hands. The other NPCs moved toward the wizard as well, each with a different weapon in their hands.

Mirthrandos laughed, then waved her staff in the air. A sparkling barrier of purple light formed between the wizard and NPCs. "Take your toys and go. I will no longer tolerate your presence in my city. Begone."

Fixit stared up at the wizard for a moment, then turned his gaze back to Watcher and Planter as a tiny metallic tear tumbled from his eye. One of the wolves moved noiselessly to Fixit's side, nuzzling the little creature with its iron snout.

"We *will* stop the withers, with or without your help," Watcher growled.

"That's great." Mirthrandos gave him a look of contempt. "Tell me all about it as you leave my city, because in three minutes, I'm releasing the golems. If you're still here by then, it'll go poorly for you and your friends. Now GET OUT!"

The chamber rang with echoes of her enraged voice.

"Come on, everyone. We have Minecraft to save, and not even a cowardly wizard who's forgotten what's important will stop us." Watcher gave Mirthrandos one last glare, then turned and headed for the stairs, the rest of the NPCs following close behind.

As they stormed out of the Weapons Vault, Watcher could hear Fixit squeaking in frustration and sadness behind them. He glanced over his shoulder at the little mechanized creature, and Fixit raised his hand into the air, fingers spread wide, then clenched it into a fist, shining iron tears tumbling down his cheeks and clinking onto the ground.

CHAPTER 21

Krael floated across the treetops, his blackened body like a shadowy hole in the sky. The sun was high overhead, its bright square face shining down upon the landscape, brightening the treetops. But the rays of light did nothing to brighten the withers; their dark skin seemed to suck in the light, giving nothing back in return.

"Kora, did you see the look on their faces when we burst through the top of that tower?" The wither king smiled at his wife.

"Yes, Krael. They were a little bit scared."

"A *little* scared?" Krael chuckled. "They were terrified."

"Who was that old woman?" Kora asked.

"How should I know?" Krael glanced over his shoulder at the rest of the army; they were following obediently behind.

"I know who it was," a high-pitched voice said.

Krael turned toward the sound. The little wither, Kobael, was floating below him.

"What are you saying?" Krael asked.

"I know who she is," the tiny wither said. "I remember her from before the Cave of Slumber."

"You do? Then tell me, fool; don't just keep it to yourself."

"Her name is Mirthrandos." Kobael's voice shook with fear under the wither king's glare. "She's the caretaker of Wizard City."

"How do you know anything about this wizard?" Kora asked skeptically.

"Well . . ." Kobael hesitated, weaving around the branches of a tall spruce tree.

"Tell us!" Krael snapped.

Kobael sighed. "She saved my life during the Great War. A couple of wizards cornered me against the wall of a cave and were about to kill me, but Mirthrandos tried to convince the other wizards that I wasn't a threat. After all, look at me."

He rose a little higher, gesturing at himself. "I'm not a threat to anyone. I'm not very strong or clever. My flaming skulls are weak, and I can't fly very fast. I'm the most pathetic wither that ever existed. Mira tried to convince the other wizards to let me go."

"Mira?" Krael's voice sounded suspicious.

"What happened?" Kora descended so as to fly next to the little wither, leaving the others in the army shocked by the unheard-of gesture.

"She blasted a hole in the wall of the cave, allowing me to escape while she created some kind of image that made it seem as if I were still there. You see, that's her magic: casting images that can trick others."

"She must have made the Valley of Arrows camouflage that covers Wizard City," Krael said, beginning to understand.

Kobael nodded. "Probably."

"What did the wizards do to her when they realized she'd let you escape?" Kora asked.

Kobael shrugged. "I would have thought they'd kill her for releasing me, but she's still alive." The little wither glanced at Kora. "How's that possible? Withers naturally have long lives because of the spells used to create us, but why would Mira also live so long?"

"It's obvious." Krael's voice boomed across the forest

beneath them. "She was given eternal life. It takes powerful magic to do that. This Mirthrandos must have done something important to be granted such a reward. We must be cautious of her."

Kora nodded.

Kobael did not respond, but just moved farther from Krael.

"Husband, did you notice she did not fight in the tower?" Kora floated back up to her husband's side. "She left the villagers to defend themselves. Perhaps she is a coward."

"She's no coward," Kobael blurted out, then cringed and slowly descended.

"What did you say?" the wither king asked, furious at the contradiction.

"Nothing . . . my king," the little wither stammered nervously.

Krael veered around the thick trunk of a towering oak, ignoring the strange monsters hiding in the foliage and chittering away as he passed.

"Tell me what you mean." There was danger in the king's voice.

Kobael sighed again, then spoke. "I saw her during the Great War. Mira—I mean Mirthrandos—is a great wizard, not a coward." Kobael lowered his three heads in shame.

"A great wizard, huh?" Krael considered these words. "This is important information. You are proving useful over and over again, even though you *are* pathetically small and weak." He glanced at his wife. "Kora, we will watch for this wizard, Mirthrandos, and if we see her again, we'll destroy her before she can use her powers or that staff of hers."

Krael smiled evilly. "I doubt her immortality will protect her from my flaming skulls. The living weapons made during the Great War are stronger than any enchantment that old wizard can create, and we are the greatest of those weapons. I'm sure our flaming skulls will take care of this Mirthrandos."

"But she—" Kobael tried to explain, but he was silenced by Krael's angry glare.

"Kobael, when you see this wizard again, you are to tell me immediately. I'll take care of her." Krael smiled as he imagined the wizard's inevitable destruction.

"But—"

"Enough. Go away, little wither; your presence bothers me." The wither king glared at Kobael.

With a sigh, the tiny monster descended lower and fell back, merging into the army of withers again.

"Don't you think you were a little too hard on that wither?" Kora asked.

"There can be no place for mercy in our army." Krael's voice boomed loud, causing the strange creatures in the treetops to go quiet. "Withers are ruthless and show no mercy . . . all must remember that."

Krael turned and glared at Kobael, and the little wither nodded. Three smiles crept across the wither king's skulls.

"When we find that wizard, we will destroy her, but first, we'll go through the portals and turn the Far Lands to ash. Then we'll return here and do the same." Krael laughed. "With these portal keys, we can go to every world and crush the last remnants of hope from all of Minecraft."

The wither king turned and flew backward, gazing upon his army. "We have rested long enough. Withers, it is time for speed. Follow me southward, toward the portals. Soon, we will claim the Far Lands for ourselves. It will be known as the Wither Lands when we're done with it."

The other withers cheered.

"Scouts, spread out and watch for our enemies. We don't want any surprises."

Dark monsters floated off in all directions, moving at high speed.

"The rest of you, follow me!" Krael shouted.

The withers cheered again, some of them shooting their flaming skulls into the treetops in excitement, ignoring the pained shouts of the creatures hiding in the foliage. Krael heard the suffering of the strange monsters and smiled, their misery making him happy.

"Soon, all will suffer, and the task I was given when the wizards created me will be complete." Krael grinned cruelly. "Soon, we will end this war, for we will have destroyed everyone!"

The withers cheered again as they followed their leader, pride in each monster's six eyes . . . all except the littlest amongst them.

An expression of fear covered Kobael's three faces as he moved farther to the back, away from the king of the withers.

CHAPTER 22

"I can't believe Mirthrandos wouldn't come with us," Blaster said. "I'm surprised a wizard can also be a coward."

"I don't think it was fear," Planter said. "She's endured more than anyone should ever have to during her eternal life. I think she's so bitter toward the wizards who punished her with immortality that she no longer wants to be any part of the world of the living."

"Well, still, I wouldn't mind her being there when we face the withers," Blaster said. "I bet she has a few tricks up her sleeves that might help."

"It doesn't matter; no one back at Wizard City is going to help," Watcher said. "We'll have to do this ourselves."

"Did you see how sad Fixit was when we left?" Planter said. "The little guy cried tears of iron. It broke my heart. For a moment, I thought he was going to follow us, but when it looked at Mirthrandos to ask, the old wizard just shook her head." She paused for a moment. "I feel sorry for her. What the ancient wizards did to her was unforgivable. Eternal life comes with either eternal loneliness or eternal pain. Or both."

"But she's a wizard," Watcher objected. "She has a responsibility."

"You and your ideas about wizards." Planter sounded frustrated. "Sometimes, people can choose for themselves what they want to do. Just because they have weapons or abilities, that doesn't make them any different from anyone else. It's the person that's important, not the stuff they have!"

Her face became a visage of anger and frustration, the entire top half of her body getting brighter and brighter as magical power built up within.

"Planter, you're holding in a lot of magical power right now," Watcher said, holding his hands in the air, to be unthreatening. "You need to release it before you hurt someone."

She glanced down at her arms; their glow cast a wide circle of lavender light, giving the forest a purple hue, and even pushing back the bright rays of the sun. A tear trickled from one of her emerald-green eyes.

"I hate this," she whispered. "I hate this power." She glanced at Watcher. "Why can't I just be me?"

"You *are*," Watcher said. "You're still Planter, but you're *also* a wizard, and we need that wizard if we're gonna stop the withers."

She glared at him, then lowered her eyes to the ground and sighed as the glow slowly faded back to its normal level. "I should be more important than my power," Planter whispered, but no one heard.

"Good job, Watcher," Blaster said. "You made her feel much better . . . not."

"What do you mean?" Watcher was confused. "I told the truth. We're gonna need Planter's powers before this is all over. If we can stop the withers from getting through the portal that leads back to the Far Lands, then we can save everyone there."

Planter cast him an angry, frustrated gaze, then slowed and moved to the back of the company.

"Perhaps compassion would be more helpful." Er-Lan moved to Watcher's side. "Planter fears magic will consume everything she loves and make her a bitter person."

"How could that happen?" Watcher didn't understand. "Magic is a powerful tool. It can help lots of people."

"Did it help the wizard, Mirthrandos?" The zombie gave Watcher a questioning, doubtful gaze. "That wizard is consumed with hatred for the others who punished her. If magic had not been involved, it is likely Mirthrandos could have lived a normal life. Instead, the punishment forced this wizard to watch all loved ones die." He swerved around a tall oak tree, then stopped and looked straight up, the zombie's claws slowly extending from his fingertips.

"What is it?" Watcher pulled out a normal bow and notched an arrow. He aimed the shaft upward, in the direction Er-Lan was staring.

"There are things in the treetops." The zombie sniffed the air just as some leaves fluttered to the ground. "Er-Lan can smell them. They do not smell normal . . . or peaceful."

Watcher waved his bow over his head, getting the attention of the others, then spoke in a low voice as they all drew near. "Er-Lan senses something in the treetops."

"Maybe it's those strange creatures we fought before?" Mapper said. "Perhaps they followed us."

Watcher shook his head. "Can't be; that was near the Lake of Fire. We're nowhere near that forest."

"I say let 'em come down and face us." Cutter drew his diamond sword. "I can introduce them to my little friend." He pointed his blade up at the treetops.

"A battle that can be avoided is a battle that will always be won." Mapper's voice shook a little. "Perhaps this is a good time to run."

"I think he's right." Planter moved to the old man's side and glared at Watcher. "We don't have to hurt those creatures up there . . . so let's not."

"I agree," Watcher said. "Everyone took some of the potions from the Weapons Vault, right?" The NPCs all nodded. "Good; drink a potion of swiftness. We'll leave whatever's up there in the dust."

Everyone pulled out glass vials filled with a blue liquid. Watcher put his to his lips and drained the contents. The bitter taste of netherwart filled his mouth, making him want to spit the liquid out, but then the sharp sweetness of raw sugar pushed the tanginess aside. Instantly, light blue swirls, the color of the sky at noon, appeared and floated around his head.

"Come on, everyone . . . we run."

Watcher took off, heading to the southeast, swerving around trees and shrubs. The rest of the NPCs followed on his heels, their feet thundering across the forest floor. Overhead, Watcher could just barely make out the sounds of creatures running across the treetops after the group, but they weren't nearly fast enough to keep up.

The villagers sprinted through the forest, curving around oak and spruce trees, their branches towering high overhead. With the exception of their footsteps, the entire forest was completely quiet; not an animal or monster could be heard. Watcher realized he missed the sounds of unseen cows, pigs, and chickens that typically percolated through the forests of this land. *Strange that we can't hear those animals now,* he thought. But the lack of growls or snarls was a refreshing change, as well; it eased some of the tension burning within him.

Soon, their path through the woods ended atop a large hill. Below them, the forest gave way to a brightly colored mesa biome, its valleys and spires looking like they were sculpted into the landscape by an artist's gigantic hand. Bands of color decorated the hills and towers, with stripes of white, brown, tan, yellow, and rusty red stretching across the landscape as if the blocks had been put down onto the terrain in layers. Across the tops of the mesa, fields of cactus grew, their spines glistening in the afternoon sun.

At the head of the formation, Blaster slowed to a stop, the blue spirals around his body flickering for a moment, then disappearing; the potion's effect had ceased.

Watcher moved to the boy's side and stared out at the colorful biome, trying to find a path.

"What do you think?" Blaster turned and looked at him. "Do we run across the tops of the mesas and hope there's a path through the cacti, or run through the ravines?"

"It'll be faster if we just go across the tops; we can cut through the cacti," Watcher said. "Speed is more important than—"

"We'll be totally exposed up there." Planter moved next to Blaster, her eyes focused on the mesa and away from Watcher. "If any monsters see us, we'll have nowhere to hide."

"Sure, but if we—" Watcher started to say, but he was cut off.

"Running out there in the open could get some of us hurt or worse." Planter's voice was cold and emotionless. "We'll go through the narrow valleys and remain unseen."

She glanced over her shoulder, still ignoring Watcher. "Everyone, follow me." Then, without waiting for any further discussion, Planter ran down the hill.

"But . . ." Watcher wanted to talk about this strategy, but everyone was already heading down the hill after Planter.

Removing his diamond chest plate, Watcher put on the Elytra wings his sister had given him before they'd started chasing the withers across Minecraft. He took two quick steps, then jumped into the air. The wings snapped open and caught the wind, lifting him into the sky. Leaning forward, he dove toward the bottom of the hill, speeding past the other NPCs. At the last instant, he pulled up and landed gracefully on the ground, then turned and faced Planter as she approached.

"We need to talk about this plan." Watcher removed the wings and put them into his inventory, then put his diamond armor back on. "I think we should . . ."

"Running through the valleys will be less risky," Planter said dismissively as she sped past, sounding agitated.

He stood there as the rest of the party ran by, many of them giving Watcher shrugs. Er-Lan moved to his side and spoke quietly in his ear.

"This is the safest way," the zombie said. "Being unseen is always preferable."

"But I would have liked to discuss it, either way. Instead, I was just dismissed."

Er-Lan just shrugged. "Planter is wise. This is a safe plan and will keep all from harm."

"I hope so." Watcher drew the Flail of Regrets, the weapon glowing bright, pushing back the afternoon sun and lighting the two friends with an iridescent hue. "These walls are steep. If we run into any monsters down here, escape will be difficult."

"Perhaps, but the safest path is usually the best." Er-Lan gave his friend a toothy smile, his razor-sharp teeth shining in the afternoon sun, then took off running into the narrow valley, following the rest of the group.

"I hope you're right, Er-Lan," Watcher whispered to no one. "It's just . . . I have a bad feeling about this." Then, turning, he followed the zombie into the colorful valley, the Flail in his hand pulsing with magical power, as if it were trying to warn him about something . . . but what?

CHAPTER 23

The villagers sprinted through the valleys that wove through the mesa landscape. Watcher continually glanced upward, checking the direction of the clouds as they drifted from east to west overhead, hoping to see they were continuing southward, but the circuitous paths of the steep valleys made it difficult to keep a constant bearing, especially when the valleys cut across other narrow ravines.

The choice of which to take was difficult each time; because of the curving nature of the paths, they couldn't tell initially if the ones they followed would continue to the south. Many times, they had to double back when they ran into a dead end or the path turned to the east or north, taking the NPCs away from their destination. However, after going back several times, and losing much of the day, they seemed to finally be on a good path leading toward their goal: the distant portal.

Suddenly, a growling sound filled the air behind them. Watcher glanced over his shoulder, but could only see the brown and tan and red and yellow layers of the valley wall. They'd just turned a corner and couldn't see very far behind them.

"Hey . . . Blaster . . . you hear something?" Watcher tried to keep his voice low so as to not alarm the others.

Blaster slowed and allowed Watcher to catch up.

"What did you say?"

Just then, another growl echoed off the valley walls.

"I asked if you heard that." Watcher glanced at Blaster and could see tiny square goosebumps spreading across his arms. "I'm guessing you did?"

The boy nodded as he removed his black leather armor and replaced it with a rich brown set. He drew his two razor-sharp curved knives as the expression on his face changed from his normal jovial-Blaster expression to his grim, determined battle-face.

"Cutter, monsters behind us," Watcher called out, and the big NPC glanced back at him just as more growls floated through the narrow valley.

Suddenly, the sound of many feet trampling the ground filled the air. A huge mob of horrific creatures, like the mismatched monsters from the forest near the Lake of Fire, turned the corner and advanced toward the group.

"Everyone, take up defensive positions." Watcher's voice boomed off the earthen walls, amplified by his magic. He pulled out the Fossil Bow of Destruction and drew back the string. "Blaster . . . healing potions." He grunted with pain as the Bow reached out for his HP and tore it from his body, powering the weapon's enchantments.

The monsters charged just as Watcher released the bowstring. The arrow streaked through the air and hit the lead monster. It was a huge spider with two zombie arms and a zombie head. An expression of surprise and shock covered the creature's face as the magical arrow took all of its HP.

Agony flowed across Watcher's body as if he were on fire. He was about to say something when a splash potion shattered across his back, pushing the pain back to a manageable level. He pulled back on the string and fired again, destroying a skeleton-zombie thing.

Arrows from the other NPCs tore into the front ranks, but did little to stop the advancing horde. Watcher kept firing as fast as he could, eliminating a monster with each shimmering shaft. It was enough to slow their charge, but the creatures still advanced.

"They aren't slowing down!" someone shouted.

"What do we do? Should we run? Should we run?"

"Hold your ground!" Watcher shouted as pain erupted from every nerve. He fired the Bow of Destruction again and again, this time aiming for monsters at the rear of the horde. The magical arrows tore through the monsters at the front to reach their targets, felling many. But he still just wasn't doing enough damage. More terrifying creatures were filing into the valley, likely coming from the forest they had just left.

And then an idea materialized in Watcher's head. "Cutter, Blaster, take NPCs up on the valley walls."

"But if we leave you down here, you'll be overrun," Blaster said.

"Just do it. When you're high enough, use the magic bows from the Vault."

"But if we use them now, we won't have them for the withers." Mapper sounded terrified.

"Well, if we don't stop these monsters here and now, then they'll harass us all the way to the portal." Pain slashed at Watcher's HP as he fired the Bow of Destruction again. "Use the magic bows." He fell to one knee as Er-Lan poured a potion of healing across his back, the zombie careful to stay away from the liquid, which was poisonous to the undead.

Blaster and Cutter nodded, then took off, each taking a group of warriors, leaving just a small contingent with Watcher.

"The rest of you, go with Blaster and Cutter," Watcher said. "I'll stay here and keep the monsters occupied."

"But if they—"

"Just go!" Watcher shouted, his voice sounding like thunder, his body glowing bright with iridescent power.

The villagers stepped back, then followed Blaster and Cutter, leaving Watcher alone to face the horde. Reaching into his inventory, he pulled out a potion of healing and set it on the ground before him, then pulled back on the Bow of Destruction and fired it again, aiming at a monster at the rear of the formation.

The monsters, seeing Watcher now stood alone in the narrow valley, snarled and growled savagely, then charged straight at him. Fear pulsed through his body as the oncoming wave of fangs and claws glistened in the afternoon sunlight.

Suddenly, Planter was at his side, her shield blazing with purple flames. "I hate this magic." She glared at him. "You keep making me use it, even if I don't want to."

"Just fall back and leave me here, alone."

The monsters were getting closer.

"You know I'm not gonna do that." Planter tensed her body, then lunged toward the angry horde. Her armor flashed, sending a wave of bright light at the monsters, washing across their strange, mutated bodies. The mob stopped their charge, just six blocks away, confused.

Watcher glanced at the sides of the valley. Cutter and Blaster were both in position.

"Open Fire!" he shouted, his booming voice echoing off the walls of the valley.

Instantly, a wave of arrows streaked down at the monsters, five sparkling shafts flying from each bow. The magical projectiles hit the swarm of monsters, tearing into their HP. The NPCs fired again and again before the magical weapons crumbled to dust, their magic consumed. As each bow vanished, the NPCs pulled more from their inventories and kept attacking.

"Keep firing!" Watcher shouted as he drew back on his bowstring and fired, ignoring the pain raging through his body. The NPCs attacked again and again, the multitude of enchanted arrows like a lethal rain. The horrific monsters shouted in pain and fright, but started moving forward again, driven by some need to destroy.

The villagers pulled more magical bows from their inventories as Watcher continued to fire the Bow of Destruction. From both sides of the valley, death fell upon the monsters, reducing their numbers even more.

"That's enough with the bows," Watcher shouted; the monsters were getting closer. "Draw swords."

Putting the Bow of Destruction back into his inventory, he drew the Flail of Regret. "You ready, Baltheron?" The flail flashed once, then glowed bright. "Everyone . . . CHARGE!"

Watcher sprinted at the enemy host, the spiked ball and chain swinging over his head. With all his strength, he swung the weapon at his foes. The Flail smashed through multiple bodies, causing each to flash red. Before they could recover, he attacked again, carving a path of destruction through the monsters' ranks. Creatures tried to leap on top of him, but flaming arrows streaked through the air and hit their hideous bodies, knocking them away; Planter was watching his back.

Gathering his magic, Watcher forced it into the Flail of Regrets, making it glow brighter and brighter with power. The monsters saw the iridescent glare and moved back, afraid, but by now the other NPCs were at the creatures' backs. They fell upon the terrified monsters, their new enchanted swords and axes and spears from the Weapons Vault ripping the monsters' HP from their bodies.

Suddenly, a small figure leaped high into the air and landed amidst the monsters; it was Blaster. He held the two long, curved swords from Wizard City, each glowing bright with magical power. He spun to the right, then to the left, the blades becoming a whirlwind of destruction around him. Monsters tried to reach him with their claws and fangs, but the enchanted weapons pushed them back as their razor-sharp edges caused the creatures to flash red with damage over and over.

Watcher drove forward, the spiked flail throwing monsters to the left and right. Cutter appeared next to Blaster, a magical battle axe in his strong grip. The three of them crushed the monsters while the rest of the army formed a ring, trapping the creatures in a circle of death. In seconds, it was over; the last of the monsters had perished.

"I love these swords." Blaster pointed at Cutter. "But I don't think I like them as much as you like your new battle axe, right?"

The big NPC smiled and nodded, looking down at the huge, enchanted weapon as the rest of the group laughed.

Watcher turned and found Planter standing with Fencer and Mapper. They were pulling out potions of healing and handing them out; some of the villagers were badly wounded, their HP critically low. Many fell to their knees, groaning in pain, but the soothing effects of the healing potions quickly had them on their feet again.

"Planter, thanks for watching my back," Watcher said. "I knew it was your flaming arrows keeping me safe."

"I would have done it for anyone." Planter's voice was completely devoid of emotion.

Watcher sighed.

"We need to get moving," Cutter said.

Just then, the growls and moans of more monsters filled the air.

"If we stay in these valleys, we're done for." Cutter glanced at Watcher expectantly. "It sounds as if there's a lot of monsters down here. We need another plan."

Watcher nodded and climbed up the valley wall. At the top, where a nice open plateau should have been, a field of cacti grew instead, their razor-sharp spines glistening in the sunlight. The entire plateau was covered with the prickly plants, making it impossible to pass. Watcher drew an axe and chopped at a cactus. He quickly destroyed it, but the sound was easy to hear.

"If we chop through the cactus, the monsters will hear us," Blaster said. "They'll fall on us from behind and we'll be trapped out there in the cactus. I don't like that idea very much."

"I have a different sort of idea," Watcher said, motioning for the other NPCs to approach. They climbed the steep wall of the valley until they all stood next to the seemingly endless cactus forest. "Everyone get ready to run," Watcher said.

"Through that?" Planter pointed at the spines before her, an angry expression on her face. "What are you thinking?"

Watcher sighed heavily, then drew the Fossil Bow of Destruction from his inventory. "The closest way out of this mesa biome is to the south, toward that strange forest in the distance." Watcher knelt and aimed to the south, then pulled back on the Bow's string. Instantly, he grunted as pain spread through his body. "Everyone ready?"

Not waiting for an answer, Watcher released the arrow. The magical shaft streaked through the bottom of the cacti, destroying the plants in a line straight ahead, making a pathway. Before anyone could move, Watcher fired again and again, widening the path. Standing, he put the bow back into his inventory, then pulled out his last golden apple and quickly ate it. His HP instantly began to rejuvenate.

" It's time to run. . . . Let's go!" Watcher sprinted across the mesa, leaving the valleys and monsters behind.

"I like it," Blaster said. "A plan from Watcher that doesn't involve fighting a massive army of monsters." He laughed, then fell in next to his friend, the rest of the NPCs following close behind.

None of them saw the dark figure floating in the treetops to the south . . . its six watching eyes filled with hatred.

CHAPTER 24

They were heading to the east, the setting sun bathing the backs of the withers with an angry red hue.

"Why are we heading this way, husband?" Kora asked. "Isn't the portal to the south?"

"It is, but there are some groups of monsters in this direction. We need to start building our army in preparation for the destruction of the Far Lands."

"I thought the withers would be destroying everything?" Three confused expressions covered Kora's faces.

"We will do much of the destruction, but we must still have troops on the ground. The monsters here will make a fantastic, expendable army." Krael smiled, then glanced at the towering trees up ahead, steering around a tall spruce. "Eventually, the villagers will realize what we are doing and will mount a defense, just like in the first Great War. Last time, we made the mistake of not having a strong enough army in place when we began our assault on the Far Lands, but this time it'll be different."

"Do you think the monsters here will fight for us?" Kora asked.

"Yes, they'll fight for us . . . or be destroyed." The king of the withers glanced around, looking for threats. "The wizards were thoughtful enough to make this world and all of its monsters available to us. With all the portal keys I took from the Weapons Vault, we'll be able to move hundreds of monsters through the Hall of Planes and into the Far Lands. We'll crush the NPCs before they even realize the Great War is still raging."

Krael laughed a malicious, gleeful laugh. Ahead, smoke billowed up from a village built in the treetops. Sorrowful moans mixed with the clattering of bones and the chuckling of endermen filled the air. "I hear our first recruits up ahead."

Krael flew up to the top of the gigantic trees, then launched a trio of fireballs at the treetops, carving a hole through the leafy canopy. Passing through the opening, he floated high into the sky, his dark army blotting out the sinking sun behind him.

He stared down at a group of burning homes, the remnants of a treetop village slowly being devoured by flames. As they approached, two dozen monsters stepped out from behind the charred wreckage and stared up at the wither army.

"Monsters, it is time for you to join the Great War." Krael's voice boomed across the landscape, his words amplified by the Crowns of Skulls.

The tallest of the zombies turned and stared up at the wither king. "Why should this zombie obey a wither? This village now belongs to the monsters, and the withers are not part of it."

"You are correct, friend, this village indeed seems to be yours." Krael moved closer, his eyes glowing dangerously. "But this world is mine. I am Krael, king of the withers, and I'm leading my comrades on an historic quest."

The zombie looked confused. Krael's left skull shook his head and was about to say something sarcastic when Right butted in. "You are to be commended for capturing this village, but we plan to take even more from the NPCs."

Center continued. "You can have this village to your-self, unless you also want all of the forest and the biome in which it sits."

"And the entire landscape, as far as you can see," Right added.

"And the whole world," Left said with a sneer.

"The withers seek to capture the entire world?" the zombie asked.

"No," Krael responded.

"No? This zombie is confused."

"I'm not surprised," Left said mockingly.

Right cast the rebellious skull an angry glare.

"No, not just this world," Krael continued. "We plan to capture *all* the worlds. So if you want this tiny little village, that's fine by me, but if, instead, you want to have *all* of the worlds in the Pyramid of Servers, then you must join us, for soon, the king of the withers will control everything."

The zombie stood motionless, processing the infor-mation in its tiny brain. Turning, the monster conferred with another zombie. An enderman teleported over to the monster and whispered into the creature's decaying green ear.

"I grow impatient," Krael's left skull said quietly. "Why don't we just blast them with our flaming skulls to convince them to help?"

"In time," Center whispered. "For now, we need these monsters as willing volunteers." He raised his voice so all the monsters in the village could hear. "And did I mention that while we capture all of Minecraft, we'll destroy every villager we find?"

The monsters instantly went silent as all eyes turned toward Krael.

"The withers are bringing war down upon the NPCs?" the zombie asked.

"No," Krael said firmly.

A confused expression covered the monster's scarred green face again.

"We aren't just going to war; we're exterminating all villagers. Our quest started with the Great War hundreds of years ago, and now, we're going to finish it. You can join us and be part of our army, or you can be our enemies. The choice, of course, is yours."

Krael glanced at his companions, and a group of withers floated closer to the monsters, surrounding the small group.

"We are faster than the NPCs, we are stronger, and we are smarter," Krael bragged. "We will destroy them."

"But . . . how can we get to the Far Lands?" the zombie asked. "Many of my zombie brothers have gone through the portals and never returned."

"Those zombies were killed by the treachery of the wizards." As the zombie processed the information, Krael smiled, then pulled out a portal key and tossed it to the green monster.

Reaching down with a clawed hand, the zombie lifted the glittering amulet off the leafy block and held it up for the other monsters to see. The deep-red light from the setting sun made the Amulet of Planes glitter and sparkle as if covered with precious rubies, the artifact pulsing with magical power.

"The portals were designed to only let creatures *in*, not *out*. But with these portal keys, we'll be able to go anywhere we please." Krael's voice was filled with pride. "I have hundreds of these keys, and with them, my army will flow through the portals like an unstoppable flood. The NPCs will never know what hit them until it is too late. We cannot lose."

The wither king moved closer to the monster, his eyes glowing even brighter, showing he was ready to attack. "Choose your fate, zombie. Are you part of my army or not?"

The zombie glanced at the other monsters, then nodded his head, the other monsters doing the same.

Krael's eyes dimmed as he relaxed. "Excellent. It's time to leave this village. You'll lead us to the next group of monsters. We'll add to our forces as we approach the portals. When our army is big enough, we'll pass through to the Far Lands and watch them burn."

The other withers laughed with glee, as did the new monstrous recruits. The only person not laughing was Kobael; a terrified expression settled across his ashen faces.

"But before we start our campaign of destruction, there is a task that must be done." Krael moved closer to the monsters. "Some of you will search for our enemy. A boy-wizard with a small company of NPC warriors follows us. Most of you will go out and hunt these villagers; when you find him, send an enderman to me and tell me his location."

The zombie nodded, then glanced at a group of skeletons and spiders; the bony creatures climbed atop the fuzzy black spiders, their bows held at the ready. Then, the spiders, with their riders on their backs, climbed down the trunks of the trees as a small group of endermen teleported to the forest floor. The creatures disappeared into the dimming landscape, the setting sun casting a deep, blood-red glow as day faded to night.

"Excellent. The rest of you, follow me." Krael's voice boomed across the treetops.

The withers descended through the hole in the treetops while the monsters used stairs built into the trunk of the tree to reach the ground. In a minute, Krael's new army of monsters was trudging through the darkening forest, heading southward toward the next village, where the monsters would be eager to join Krael's army whether they knew it now or not.

CHAPTER 25

Watcher wove around the short, stubby dark oak trees, the cool temperature of the forest a welcome relief compared to the heat of the mesa. Instead of the sounds of monsters growling and snarling, the NPCs were treated to the noises of birds squawking amongst the branches and leaves. The birds reminded him of the parrots that had helped him and his friends defeat the skeleton warlord.

It seemed like that happened a million years ago. Back then, Watcher had been a scared boy who struggled for acceptance and yearned to be someone important; he'd been so young back then. Now, the responsibility for everyone following him laid heavy on his soul, the stress of it, at times, making his head ache with worry.

"Look, the forest is ending." Blaster pointed to the edge of the biome up ahead.

Watcher looked ahead, slowing his movement as he curved around another dark oak tree, its trunk two blocks across, the dark branches stretching out as if trying to block out the silvery light of the rising moon in the east.

"I'm gonna miss the sounds of all those birds when we leave this forest," Mapper said.

Watcher glanced over his shoulder and smiled at the old man. "Me too."

"I have to say, this is the strangest dark oak forest I've ever seen," Blaster said. "I'm used to having all these branches connecting together, making a solid roof of leaves, but instead, they're all spaced out."

"It's as if someone cut down every other tree," Mapper added.

"Who cares?" Cutter moved next to the old man's side. "I'm just glad there weren't a lot of monsters in this forest. Letting sunlight down onto the forest floor probably dissuaded any zombies or skeletons from spawning."

"Look up ahead," Planter said. "There's something strange about the landscape."

Watcher looked where she was pointing. Their path was taking them into a savanna biome, with rolling hills covered in long grass and distorted acacia trees dotting the landscape. Each tree was bent and twisted into a different shape, which was normal for a savanna biome, but the trees in this terrain seemed sickly and ancient. Long vines hung down from the branches of each tree, almost reaching the ground.

Watcher stepped into the strange biome just as the moon rose high enough to cast its silvery light upon the terrain. The tall grass lacked its normal pale-green hue; instead, it was almost devoid of color, the long blades shaded a bland gray. The leaves on the trees were the same color as the grass, making the twisted acacia trees seem as if they came from a child's drawing. The only things with any color at all were the thorny vines drooping off the branches.

"Er-Lan does not like the look of the vines." The zombie pointed with a scarred hand, a claw extended from each finger.

"Yeah, I agree," Watcher said. "The thorns on those things look painful."

Er-Lan grunted his agreement.

"You notice the grass isn't moving?" Blaster stepped around a small shrub and pointed to the ground.

"So?" Watcher reached down and moved his fingers through the gray strands, then glanced up at Blaster, confused.

"No wind."

"How's that possible?" Watcher asked, realizing how strange it was. "There's always a breeze moving from east to west everywhere in Minecraft."

"But there's a more important question," Blaster said, drawing one of the enchanted, curved swords from the Weapons Vault. "If there's no wind, why are the vines moving?"

Watcher stared at the closest vines. Now that he looked closely, he could see that they squirmed and writhed like living creatures, their thorns sparkling under the light of the crescent moon. "I really don't like those things now."

Reaching into his inventory, Watcher pulled Needle from his inventory with his right hand, then grabbed a typical wooden shield with his left. It wasn't enchanted, like Planter's; it was just a piece of wood held together with metal bands. Having Needle's keen edge at hand made him feel a little better, but he still gave the vines a wide berth.

Off to the right, Watcher spotted Planter walking by herself. He moved to her side.

"Hi."

She just grunted a reply.

"You really saved me back there in that narrow canyon."

She didn't reply.

"If you hadn't protected me with your shield, I would have probably been hurt . . . or worse. It's quite some trick you can do with that thing."

"A trick? A *trick*?!" Planter glared at him. "You know how it feels when I'm using that stupid shield?"

Watcher shook his head.

"It feels like my mind is getting pulled into the shield and I'm losing part of myself. *It* wants me to become someone different, someone I don't know." She looked back at the ground. "I hate it."

She's feeling the maker of the shield, Needle's creator, Dalgaroth, said. *She's feeling the tiny fragment of soul from the shield's creator, Sotaria.*

"Planter, Needle tells me you're feeling—"

I'm not Needle; I'm Dalgaroth, the greatest sword-smith who ever walked the planes of Minecraft.

"Sorry . . . um . . . he says he's not Needle, he's Dalgaroth." Watcher held the sword up, feeling a little dumb apologizing to a sword, but he did it again. "Sorry."

He lowered the blade and glanced at Planter. "Anyway, Dalgaroth says you're probably feeling the creator of the shield; her name was Sotaria. You're probably feeling her presence through your magic."

She raised her eyes to Watcher. "It feels as if I'm going insane every time I use that stupid shield."

There's only the smallest sliver of Sotaria's mind in the shield, Dalgaroth said. *Her mind was split up into many shields. Only by bringing all the shields together can her consciousness be merged together again.*

"Dalgaroth said—"

"I know what he said; that dumb sword invaded my mind and spoke to me at the same time as he was blabbing to you."

"You're upset about Dalgaroth talking to you?" Watcher asked.

"I don't like having my mind being invaded by them." She glared at the sword in Watcher's hand. "When I have a thought, I want to know it's mine, not something one of *them* put in my head." She glanced at Watcher. "You should think about that. All these ancient wizards cared about was power; they'll do anything to get more."

What your friend says is true, Dalgaroth said. *There were many among us who were reckless and caused great harm in their pursuit of power. There were even rumors a long time ago that suggested some of the wizards created the warlocks in their quest for power, but their creations got away from them.*

"You see? They can't be trusted," Planter said.

"I'm sure Dalgaroth and the others in the weapons are different." Watcher glanced down at Needle. "Isn't that right?"

Watcher speaks true; the worst of us perished during the war. They forgot their role and were destroyed by their greed.

"What do you mean, 'their role?'" Watcher asked.

Wizards were the strongest and most powerful amongst the villagers back in the old days. With that power comes the responsibility to protect others and watch out for them, but some of the wizards forgot this and focused their attention inward, rather than looking to help others. It drove many insane. The last of us chose this path: putting our minds and magical powers into weapons that could be wielded by the greatest NPC warriors, forever removing the temptation of gaining more power.

"Until now." Planter pointed at Watcher. "All you care about is power . . . just like *them.*"

"That's not true." It felt as if she'd stabbed him in the heart. "I just want to protect our friends and family, and I can't do that with these skinny, weak arms." He held his sword up in the air. "Without these magical weapons, we'd have lost to the zombie warlord long ago. Without Needle and these other enchanted tools, we couldn't have defeated the skeleton and spider warlords. These weapons helped us to do things we would have thought impossible."

"And now look where they got us." Planter scowled, anger furling her unibrow. "We have a massive army of withers trying to destroy everything. Great work, Watcher."

The accusation was like an anvil crushing his soul.

Did I really cause this? Watcher thought. *Is this all my fault? Dalgaroth, tell me, is it my fault?*

Some questions are best answered alone, but one thing I can tell you is—oh no . . . trouble coming.

Watcher glanced up just in time to see an arrow speeding toward his head. Before he could even think, Needle flashed through the air and knocked the projectile aside faster than Watcher even thought possible.

An enderman stepped out from behind a large grass-covered hill nearby and pointed with a dark fist. "There are the villagers. Get them!"

A group of ten spider jockeys moved out from behind the hill. The weak moonlight made the dark spiders difficult to see, but the skeletons riding atop the fuzzy black monsters were easy to spot. The mob charged straight at them, the spiders clicking their mandibles together excitedly as the skeletons sent their pointed shafts at the NPCs.

"Shields!" Watcher shouted. He held his up just as three arrows hammered into the wooden surface.

Villagers shouted out in pain as some of the arrows found their mark, but soon arrows were flying back at the monsters, the dark spiders trying to knock the NPCs' shots out of the air.

"Form a line," Cutter shouted, taking charge of the battle. The big NPC shouted out more commands, but Watcher ignored him; he wanted to find the enderman.

Suddenly, a strange chuckling sound floated across the savanna from behind him. Turning, Watcher found two purple eyes staring at him from the darkness. The eyes bored into him for a second, then turned from lavender to harsh white. The enderman opened its mouth wide and screeched, then charged.

Watcher swung Needle at the monster, only to have the enderman disappear, then materialize behind him. A dark fist slammed into his back, knocking him to the ground. Rolling across the pale grass, Watcher stood and faced the monster. It charged again, then disappeared as soon as it was within arms' reach. This time, the young wizard was ready; he spun around and swung Needle with all his strength, slashing at where he thought the dark creature would materialize. The sharp edge of his blade sliced across the monster's midsection, taking its HP. The enderman flashed red as it took damage, then disappeared in a cloud of purple particles.

"You need some help over there?" Blaster shouted.

Watcher glanced over his shoulder. The NPCs were trading arrows with the skeletons, but the spiders were moving so quickly, it was hard to hit the bony targets.

A whooshing noise filled the air. Watcher recognized the sound and ducked, then spun, slicing through the air around him. Needle found dark flesh again as it crashed into the monster's legs, making the enderman screech in pain. Then, before it could teleport away, Watcher dove toward the creature, his enchanted blade glowing bright with magical power. The keen edge came down upon the monster before it knew what was happening, taking the last of its HP. The enderman disappeared, a surprised and frightened expression on its dark face, leaving behind three glowing balls of XP and a greenish ender pearl.

"You won't be reporting our location to Krael and the other withers now." Watcher smiled, scooped up the pearl and XP, then ran toward his friends.

As he approached, another enderman suddenly appeared behind Watcher and sent its dark fists smashing into the back of his head. He staggered for a moment, then turned and swung at the creature. It smiled at him and disappeared, then materialized behind him again. Before the dark creature could attack, Planter charged at the terrifying monster, her shield held before her. She shoved into it, the wood and metal rectangle bursting with purple fire; the enderman glared at the flames, then teleported away, leaving the rest of the monsters to the battle.

A zombie charged at Planter, but before it could get

near, Blaster streaked by, wielding his new enchanted curved swords. He slashed at the monster, carving away at its HP until it disappeared with a pop, a confused expression on its scarred face.

"Er-Lan . . . look out!" Mapper shouted.

Watcher turned and watched in horror as a pair of spiders charged toward his zombie friend. Running as fast as he could, Watcher sprinted toward Er-Lan, but knew he'd never reach him in time.

Just as the spiders reached out with their wicked, curved claws, Er-Lan became completely still and closed his eyes. Suddenly, the ground heaved upward as if struck by a gigantic meteor. Gray blocks of grass thrust up in a wave, throwing the spiders into the air, then moving outward and hitting the other monsters. Skeletons tumbled from the backs of the spiders, many of them getting trampled by the dark fuzzy creatures. Some bony riders were tossed in the air, flashing red when they landed on the ground with a thud. Surprisingly, none of the NPCs seemed affected; the destructive wave passed only across the monsters' position.

In the confusion, Watcher charged at the monsters, yelling at the top of his voice, "CHARGE!"

The NPCs fell upon the monsters with their new enchanted weapons. Cutter's huge battle axe made quick work of the spiders while the enchanted spears, swords, and warhammers of the others shattered the skeletons' HP. Monstrous shouts of surprise and fear filled the air as the monsters perished until a cold silence spread across the battlefield. A lone enderman had survived the battle, the dark monster standing a dozen blocks away. The monster glared at Watcher, then disappeared in a cloud of lavender mist.

"You can be sure that enderman is gonna tell Krael where we are," Blaster said.

"It doesn't matter," Cutter said. "He knows we're heading for the portal, same as the wither army. It's a race that I'm planning on winning. Let's get moving."

"Sure, but first, what was that earthquake that tossed the monsters into the air?" Watcher turned to Planter. "Did you do that?"

She shook her head. "The last thing I want is *more* magical abilities."

"I don't think I did it." Watcher glanced at his companions, waiting for someone to speak up, saying they had used some kind of weapon taken from the Weapons Vault, but all remained silent. "Strange . . . maybe I have more powers than I even realize."

Blaster rolled his eyes.

Watcher moved to Er-Lan's side and put a hand on his shoulder. "Well, however it happened, it came just in time. Those spiders were about to get you."

Er-Lan nodded and looked away, his body tense.

"We don't have time to stand around," Mapper said. "I think it'd be best if we were moving."

"I agree," Blaster said. "Let's go."

Watcher nodded and headed to the southeast, toward the distant portals. But as he ran, he glanced back at Er-Lan. Something about his friend seemed wrong, as if he were in the midst of some internal struggle. As he looked at the zombie, a hand suddenly pushed him to the side, causing him to narrowly miss running into an acacia tree, the thorny vines reaching out to him.

"Maybe you should look forward while you're running?" Blaster said with a smile. "You wizards have all this magical power, but can't even run in a straight line without hitting something." He shook his head and laughed, then slapped Watcher on the back.

Watcher smiled back, then motioned for Er-Lan to follow. The zombie took an uncertain step forward, then another and another until he finally started to run, his eyes focused on the ground and away from Watcher.

"Come on, everyone, we sprint to the portals." Watcher's voice boomed across the landscape, amplified by his magic.

Before anyone could reply, he took off, running as fast as he could, though he knew they were heading toward the greatest and most dangerous battle of his life.

CHAPTER 26

An uncomfortable silence spread across the company as they ran through the gray savanna. Everyone in the party felt the tension. It wasn't because of the withers who wanted to destroy them, or the monsters they'd just defeated; no, it was because of Planter and Er-Lan. The tension etched deep into their faces showed internal battles were taking place within both of them. Watcher didn't understand what was really going on, and had no idea how to help. It was obvious there was some problem here, but until he knew what to do, he figured it was best to remain quiet.

He understood Planter's struggle. She'd used her magic during the battle, saving Watcher, again, and he knew she hated it. Planter didn't want to be a wizard and was afraid she'd lose herself to the power flowing through her veins. Watcher could understand that; he was afraid of it too, but with the withers trying to destroy everything he cared about, he knew he had to take the risk. With Er-Lan, though, he had no idea what was wrong.

Something had scared or shocked the zombie during that last battle. Watcher had no idea what had frightened

Er-Lan; maybe it was that strange earthquake . . . who knew?

"Watcher, do you have a plan when we reach the portal?" Mapper asked.

"Why don't we rest for a minute?" Watcher slowed to a walk, then stopped.

The stars overhead sparkled like fine gems sewn into a dark tapestry. Glancing up at the glittering show overhead, Watcher could almost imagine he was home, in the Far Lands. The illusion didn't last very long; a thorny vine slithered across the ground and tried to grab a rabbit running past. The furry creature screeched in fright, then hopped away.

Watcher led them into a small recession, free from the strange trees and their living vines, and they sat down to rest. Both Er-Lan and Planter sat next to each other, off to the side, away from any unwanted questions. Watcher glanced at them, their eyes downcast, and sighed, then explained his plan.

"Here's what I was thinking: if you remember, the portal is located on a mushroom island."

The NPCs all nodded.

"But there isn't much cover there to help fight the withers. So I figured we'd make our stand in the biome next to it."

"You mean that strange, distorted forest?" Blaster asked.

"Exactly." Watcher lowered his voice. "We'll build steps so we can run to the tops of those trees and fight them while they're floating off the ground. These new enchanted weapons from the Vault will give us an advantage, too."

"But we used up a lot of the bows back in the canyons," Mapper said. "Any thoughts there?"

"Well, I thought maybe I could use the Wand of Cloning and duplicate them right before we need them."

It won't work, Baltheron said in Watcher's mind. *The wand can only duplicate mundane things; it won't replicate the complicated enchantments woven into those weapons.*

Watcher frowned.

"What is it?" Mapper asked.

"The Flail said using the Wand on the enchanted bows won't work," Planter said before Watcher could answer.

"You can hear his weapons speaking to him?" Blaster asked.

She nodded.

"Cool." Blaster smiled at her, but Planter's face remained emotionless, her gaze moving back to the ground.

"Then we'll use what we have," Watcher said, his voice full of confidence, though he knew it to be a lie. He sat on the ground next to another NPC. "We'll use the trees for cover, making the withers' flaming skulls ineffective from the air. This will force them to come down to us, near the ground. And we'll be waiting for them . . ." He glanced at Blaster. "Maybe we'll have a little explosive surprise ready for them?"

Blaster smiled. "I just need some time to get it set up."

Watcher nodded. "We have to stop them from going through the portal; the lives of all our families and everyone we've ever known depend on it."

"Excuse me for interrupting your grand, wizardly plan." Cutter stood. "But what if the withers just blow up the trees? Then we'll have no cover at all. What do you propose then?"

The big warrior sat as Watcher thought about a response . . . but he had none.

There's another way, Baltheron said.

"What?" Watcher asked.

There's another way to stop the withers from going through the portal.

Watcher pulled out the Flail of Regrets and stared at it.

"What is it?" The young wizard sounded frantic. "What can we do to stop the withers?"

Just destroy the portal, the deep voice boomed within his mind.

"Of course," Watcher and Planter said at the same time.

"What is it?" Cutter asked.

Watcher smiled. "We'll destroy the portal and trap the withers in this world."

"I like it!" Blaster exclaimed.

"We'll go through the portal, then break it from the other side, in the Hall of Planes," Watcher said.

"What about the people of this world?" Planter stood and scowled at Watcher.

"I don't see any way we can help them." Watcher could see the pain etched into Planter's face. She cared for the villagers living in this strange world and wanted to save them as well.

Watcher shook his head. "Sometimes, we can't help everyone. All we can do is the best we can. Cutter's right. If we stand and fight the withers, they'll wipe us out and then they'll go to the Far Lands and destroy everything." He sighed. "The only way is to destroy the portal and trap them in this world. That's the best we can do."

He turned and looked at each of his companions. They all were haggard and exhausted from their traumatic pursuit of Krael through this strange land, but every one of them knew they had no choice; they had to see this through to the end.

"I think it's best we started moving. With this new information from Baltheron, it's now a race to see if we can beat Krael to the portal. We'll head straight to the mushroom island."

Mapper pulled the ancient map from his inventory and pointed at the parchment with a wrinkled finger. "There's a narrow strip of land that leads to the mushroom island. We should make for that."

Watcher nodded. "I think speed is more important

right now. This is a good time to use the last potions of swiftness we took from the Vault."

The others nodded and pulled the colorful potions from their inventory. Watcher glanced at Planter and tried to give her a smile, but she kept her eyes on the horizon and away from him.

Watcher tipped the potion into his mouth. Instantly, colorful swirls appeared before his face. "Now we run, fast."

He put the Flail of Regrets back into his inventory and drew Needle, then took off, sprinting faster than he'd ever gone before. The thunder of footsteps at his back told him his friends were right behind him, all of them streaking toward the battle that would decide the fate of Minecraft.

CHAPTER 27

As the moon climbed higher into the sky, the gray savanna landscape finally ended, leaving the party in an oak and birch forest that would have seemed idyllic except for the warped and twisted appearance of everything in it. Trees, bent at strange angles, covered the landscape, the trunks and branches curved into impossible shapes. The oaks and birches here lacked any similarity to the acacia trees in the savanna; instead, these trees seemed violently distorted, as if an angry giant had clawed at the forest, trying to uproot every living thing. Watcher had no doubt some magical spell cast by the monster warlocks or NPC wizards had damaged this biome, leaving it a scarred version of its original self, the beauty of the forest forever morphed into something terrible and disturbing. This was the biome they'd entered after leaving the mushroom island when they first came through the portal and entered into this world; they were close.

Watcher wove a path around the crooked trunks and misshapen bushes, continually heading southeast. He didn't need to consult Mapper for directions; he could now hear the portal, somehow, in the back of his mind. It was speaking to him, giving him a magical warning about the portal keys. The enchanted doorway wasn't using words to warn the young wizard; rather, it was transmitting feelings of fright directly into his mind. He glanced at Planter and could tell by the worried expression on her beautiful square face that she could feel the message as well. The oppressive emotion was being broadcast from the portal, as if the suffering of every creature who tried to pass through the ring without a portal key had been recorded, and Watcher and Planter were now feeling the emotions of those doomed souls replayed over and over again.

Does it always do that? Watcher asked his enchanted weapons.

Yep, the scratchy voice of Taerian said, the Gauntlets of Life giving off a brief flash of light. *Janus—she was the wizard who made the Hall of Planes and all the portals—anyway, she thought it would be best to warn other wizards, so they didn't forget the portal keys.*

It's terrible, Watcher thought. *I can feel the pain and sorrow of everyone who was destroyed by those portals.*

"Why didn't Janus have the portal warn everyone else?" Planter scowled at Watcher angrily.

"What?"

"Your magical friend said the portal warns the wizards. Why doesn't it warn the villagers as well?"

"I don't know."

He pulled out one of the portal keys, the long, silvery chain wrapped around his neck. Holding the reflective metallic square in his hand, he glanced down at the artifact as he dashed around misshapen trees. The ruby-red crystal at the center glowed slightly; it would likely get brighter when they were closer to their goal.

"You see." Planter pointed at Watcher. "Wizards only care about wizards."

"I don't think that's fair. I'm sure they—"

But Planter steered away from the boy, then slowed and moved to the back of their formation, her face seething with anger.

As she moved away, Watcher turned and looked up just in time to see a strange clump of leaves in his path. He leapt into the air, soaring over the warped bush, the enchanted potion of swiftness causing him to go much higher than he expected. Ducking, his head just scraped the lower limbs of a tall oak tree, their leaves slapping him in the face. When he landed on the ground, he found Blaster at his side, laughing.

"You trimming the trees with your face?" Blaster smiled.

"I jumped a little too high," Watcher said, embarrassed.

"It was fun to watch; you should do it again." Blaster moved closer and lowered his voice. "What do you think our chances are of destroying the portal before the withers make it through?"

"Well . . ." A worried expression covered Watcher's face. "I think we have a good chance, and—"

"We've been friends for a long time, Watcher. I know when you're lying. Just tell me the truth."

Watcher glanced around to see if anyone was nearby, then whispered. "The withers need to be within arm's reach for our enchanted blades to do any good. I'm not sure how many of those enchanted bows we have left, but I'm sure it's not enough. We can set up some TNT traps, but as soon as they detonate, the withers will float up into the air, out of reach again. Then they can just bombard us with their flaming skulls."

"So you have some concerns?" Blaster smiled.

"'Some concerns?!'" Watcher's voice grew louder, but he instantly lowered it to a whisper. "We have to first get to the portal, and the withers will do everything they can to stop us. Then we need to destroy the portal from the other side. It's enchanted; who knows if it can even be destroyed, although Baltheron seems to think it can. And while we're trying to break the portal, the withers will be trying to come through, blasting us with their flaming skulls." He glanced at the NPCs following him.

"I don't know if there are enough of us to do the job. So, yeah, I have 'some concerns.'"

Watcher glanced at his companions to see if any were listening. Fencer glanced at him and scowled, but when her eyes fell upon Blaster she lit up with a smile. Blaster saw it and sighed. The situation made Watcher grin.

"You're enjoying my predicament, aren't you?" Blaster scowled at his friend.

Watcher just nodded, then grew serious. "We can't just step aside and let the withers go through the portal; we have to stop them somehow. I just don't know how to keep the withers distracted while we're breaking the portal."

It only takes one person to break the portal, Dalgaroth said, his high-pitched voice filling Watcher's mind.

"What?" Watcher was confused.

Planter glanced at him; she also heard the ancient wizard's words. Veering around a warped birch, she moved to Watcher's side. "What is he trying to say?"

"Yeah . . . what do you mean?" Watcher stared down at Needle.

Some of the weapons you took from the Weapons Vault were enchanted pickaxes. Dalgaroth's voice softened as if the ancient wizard was afraid others might hear. *They have enough magical power to break the portal. It will only take one or two people to destroy the iron blocks and shut the portal forever.*

"So what?" Planter's voice sounded agitated. "What are you suggesting?"

Did you hear her? Watcher thought to Needle.

Of course I heard; she's a wizard. I can hear the thoughts of all three of you.

Planter glanced at Watcher, confused. All three?

Dalgaroth continued. *Two of your strongest villagers should go through the portal and break the iron blocks while the rest of you stay behind to keep the withers busy.*

"But that means everyone that stays behind will be trapped here in this world, with the wither army." Planter shook her head. "That's not acceptable."

If you want to stop the withers, then a sacrifice will be needed. Dalgaroth's words lacked any empathy or concern.

"You see . . . that's the problem with all you wizards," Planter pointed at Watcher, not the sword, her face red with rage. "The lives of those around you aren't important; they're just a resource to be used and then discarded when no longer needed."

"That's not how I feel." Watcher swerved around an oak bent over into an arc, the treetop brushing the ground. "I'm not willing to sacrifice anyone else."

"Sacrifice?" Blaster said. "I don't like the sound of that. Who's getting sacrificed?"

"No one!" Planter and Watcher said at the same time, their voices filling the forest with thunder.

Blaster nodded. "Good . . . I guess." The boy slowed, allowing the two wizards to move ahead of the group; none of the other NPCs wanted to be near the pair.

"What do you mean, you're not willing to sacrifice *anyone else*?" Planter asked.

"Well," Watcher lowered his voice. "Maybe I can stay behind and keep Krael busy while the rest of you go through the portal and break it."

"So you mean you'll sacrifice yourself?"

"If necessary. We don't need to make that decision now, but I'm willing to do whatever it takes to keep everyone safe in the Far Lands."

Planter glared at him, a look of exasperation and hurt on her square face. "You don't get it. All that magic has gone to your head and finally turned you into an idiot."

"Finally?" Blaster interjected with a smile, then cringed when Planter glared at him.

"I won't risk anyone else," Watcher said, his tone suggesting the discussion was over.

"This is what I'm talking about." Planter's voice grew louder as her frustration built, the glow from her upper body matching her anger, getting brighter and brighter. "You wizards think life is expendable."

"Who cares, as long as it's my life?"

"I care, you idiot." A tear trickled down her cheek.

Watcher remained silent for a moment, considering his next words, then spoke, his voice barely a whisper. "Don't you get it? If I have to sacrifice myself to keep you safe, then I'll gladly do it. You're the most important thing in the world to me, and I won't let anyone hurt you."

"Maybe you need to think of another way," Planter said. "More death isn't the answer."

Watcher just shrugged.

"And you expect me to use my magic to help with this crazy plan?"

"Of course; I expect everyone to help," Watcher said. "If we get there before the withers, we can slip through the portal and destroy it before Krael and his monsters ever reach it. But if he's already there, then we'll need everyone to use everything they have to stop the withers."

"And that includes my magic?" Planter's voice was softer now, the angry glow from her body finally receding.

Watcher nodded as he curved around another distorted tree.

"Blaster, I know you've been listening," Planter said.

"Well, with you two yelling at the top of your lungs, it's hard not to." The boy smiled, his black leather armor hiding most of his face in the darkness.

"What do you think of Watcher's plan?" Planter glanced over her shoulder at the boy.

"I think it sounds better than my idea," Blaster said.

"What's your idea?"

"Well, I don't have one that doesn't involve all of us dying horrible deaths, so Watcher's plan sounds pretty good to me."

"Have you ever known any of Watcher's plans to work the way they were intended?" Planter asked.

Blaster shrugged. "No plan works perfectly in battle. The enemy always has a way of messing things up. But a bad plan is better than no plan at all. If you ask me, I think—"

"Look, there's the mushroom island," Mapper said, pointing with a crooked finger.

Watcher glanced through the forest. The blue ocean was visible between the twisted oaks, moonlight reflecting off the calm waters. Giant red and white spotted mushrooms were visible on the strange island, with tan flattop mushrooms in the distance.

Er-Lan moved next to Watcher and grabbed his arm. "Watcher, this zombie must give you something."

"What?" Watcher was confused.

"Er-Lan thinks you will need something." The zombie handed him Tharus' purple robe, the cloth creased and wrinkled from when he'd thrown it down, but the gold stitching still bright. "It is important this cape is in Watcher's inventory before the next battle."

"I don't understand, Er-Lan."

"Just take it!" Er-Lan sounded insistent.

"I don't need that stupid thing to *look* like a wizard," Watcher said. "I don't care about what I look like or what other people think. Stuff isn't more important than people. I just want everyone to be safe."

"Then trust Er-Lan and take it . . . please." The zombie looked desperate. "Every fiber of this body says Watcher will need this cape. Take it . . . please."

Watcher never had seen his friend so serious. With a nod, he took the cloak and stuffed it into his inventory.

"Thanks." Er-Lan gave him a toothy smile. "It is important because—"

Watcher raised a hand, silencing the zombie just as a cold, empty feeling washed over him, his skin forming small, square goosebumps.

"The withers are here as well . . . I can feel them."

"Where?" Blaster asked.

Suddenly, the colored swirls floating around his face dissipated as the swiftness potion's effect faded away, his pace slowing. Watcher shifted to a walk, then stopped at the edge of the forest.

"Everyone, get behind trees." He peered around the rough trunk of an oak. Far away, a dark cloud of shadows moved across the sky, blotting out the stars. One of the shadows glowed with a purple hue.

"There they are." Cutter pointed with his diamond sword. "We gotta move . . . fast."

"Cutter's right . . . everyone ready?" Watcher glanced at his companions. They all held enchanted bows in their hands, except Planter, who held her magical shield.

"Let's go, then. RUN!"

Watcher dashed out from behind the tree and crossed the open land, heading for the narrow strip of land that led to the mushroom island. Fear pulsed through every nerve, fear for himself, but more importantly, fear for all of his friends, especially Planter. He wanted to say something to her, but before he could speak a loud screech of rage cut through the air; it came from Krael.

The villagers had been spotted, and the race had begun; the prize for second place . . . death.

CHAPTER 28

Watcher sprinted as fast as he could, every nerve burning with terror. The withers shouted at the NPCs, their angry voices filled with a thirst for violence. He wanted to peek over his shoulder to see how close they were, but Watcher knew it would only slow him down a little, and right now, speed was everything. Instead, he focused on his goal: the narrow strip of land leading to the mushroom island and the glowing portal atop the hill.

Suddenly, a flaming skull streaked above him and hit the ground ahead. An explosion tore into the tiny row of stone, the blast knocking Watcher backward. More flaming skulls smashed into the ground, changing the land bridge stretching across the ocean into a crater. The water on either side quickly filled the crater, erasing the bridge from existence. Now, if they tried to cross to the mushroom island, they'd have to swim, slowing them to a crawl; they'd be easy targets for the withers.

Watcher stood and glared up at Krael just as the sun peeked over the eastern horizon, casting a warm red light upon the landscape and making the dark monsters clearly visible in the sky.

"So, wizard . . . we meet again," the wither king

hissed. "You have been an annoyance to me for far too long. Now, it's time for your destruction."

"Everyone move together." Planter pulled out her shield as the other NPCs gathered behind her. Holding it over her head, she pulled Er-Lan right next to her, then motioned for the others to get closer as well.

Krael laughed. "That won't help you this time, girl."

The wither king glared down at her, then launched a trio of flaming skulls. Instantly, Planter's shield burst with purple flames as the protective enchantment spread over the NPCs, the iridescent cocoon of magical fire protecting them, at least for now. The wither king's projectiles smashed into the shield and exploded, the sound of the blast echoing across the landscape, but doing no damage.

Planter peered around the edge of the shield and smiled at the monster.

"You think you're safe?" Krael asked. "You're a fool."

The wither king glanced over his ashen shoulder at the rest of his army. "Withers, surround them and attack."

Watcher pulled the Flail from his inventory and gripped its leather-wrapped handle with a sweaty hand. Fear rippled through his body as the dark creatures slowly formed a circle around their party.

And then the real attack began.

Flaming skulls hammered at Planter's magical shield from all sides, the sound of the blasts nearly deafening. The sheet of purple flames thickened around the NPCs as Planter struggled to pour more of her magic into the defenses, but Watcher could see she was already tiring.

More flaming skulls smashed into the shield, forcing Watcher to cover his ears. He moved to Planter's side and put an arm around her shoulders, lending his strength to his friend.

"You can do it," Watcher whispered in her ear.

"I can feel myself getting lost in the enchantments," Planter moaned. "It's as if the shield is hungry for not just my power . . . but for my mind as well. Like it's missing part of itself and wants to fill it in with me." She glanced at Watcher. "I don't know how long I can keep the shield up."

Looking up, Watcher saw the purple flames surrounding them flicker for just an instant.

"We need to attack," Cutter shouted.

The big NPC took out one of the enchanted bows from the Vault and aimed at a group of withers. Drawing the string back, he fired. Five glittering arrows leaped from the enchanted weapon, but when they hit the lavender flames, they disappeared, consumed by Planter's shield.

"Great, we can't shoot back while the shield's up."

For the first time Watcher could ever remember, Cutter sounded scared.

"Watcher, what do we do?" Mapper asked, sounding desperate.

"I'm afraid," Fencer said.

Blaster moved to her side and held his two magical swords up, ready to protect her.

"What do we do?" someone else asked.

"What's your plan, Watcher?"

"Help us . . ."

"Use your magic . . ."

Everyone in their party was terrified, but Watcher had no idea what to do. He was just as afraid as the rest of them.

Suddenly, the sounds of cows, chickens, and pigs floated into the protective shell, though no animals were visible.

"You hear it again?" Blaster said to Watcher. "Just like before."

Watcher nodded, but he didn't know what it meant.

Just then, a strange howl cut through the air. It had a metallic sound somehow, as if some kind of mechanism were producing the majestic wail.

Suddenly, all the withers began laughing, their dark skulls pointed toward the nearby forest.

"It seems your reinforcements have arrived," Krael said to the NPCs, his three skulls chuckling.

Watcher glanced toward the tree line. Running through the trees was a metallic wolf, its howl still filling the air. On the creature's back rode Fixit, the tiny little mechite's silvery hair streaming behind him as the wolf sped across the landscape.

"It's Fixit!" Fencer shouted.

"Oh no," Watcher said as one of the withers floated closer, ready to attack the mechite and wolf. "They're going to destroy him."

The wolf suddenly turned around and ran back into the woods. As they turned, Fixit glanced at Watcher, a knowing smile on his metal face, as if he knew a secret.

The wither laughed and moved closer, an expression of vicious glee on its three faces. The wolf howled again from behind the cover of the forest, but this time it was joined by another metallic voice, then another and another, and then a hundred wolves emerged from the forest, each with a mechite rider. Instead of hands, each mechite had sharp knives or hammers attached to their wrists, their weapons glistening in the morning sun.

The wither retreated, unsure what to do with all the wolves and mechites.

"Don't retreat, you fool," Krael screamed. "Attack!"

But before the wither could fire a barrage of skulls, an army of iron and obsidian golems came storming out of the forest, the ground shaking with every thunderous footstep. Along with them came more wolves sprinting across the ground, each with a mechite hanging on to their silvery fur, weapons held at the ready. Atop the lead golem sat Mirthrandos, her body ablaze with purple fire and her staff like a bolt of liquid fire, blazing with magical energy.

"Withers," the ancient wizard shouted, her voice amplified and booming like thunder. "Prepare to meet your doom!"

And the Battle for the Portal began.

CHAPTER 29

The withers formed a shadowy line in front of the approaching golems, then launched their flaming skulls. As they flew through the air, Mirthrandos launched her own assault, firing what looked to Watcher like tiny purple missiles, each one spat from the end of her glowing wooden staff. The tiny magical projectiles hit the flaming skulls, causing them to explode in mid-air and keeping them from harming any of the mechanical creatures.

"ATTACK!" the wizard screamed, her voice deafening.

The golems charged at the withers, shooting high up into the air to grab the lowest. Other golems picked up wolves and mechites and tossed them through the air, the creatures landing with incredible precision upon the shoulders of the nightmarish withers.

"Planter, you can lower your shield," Watcher said.

She gratefully complied.

"Everyone, get to the mushroom island while the withers are busy."

"We can't just leave Mirthrandos out there without any help," Planter said.

"We'll help them when we're across the water." Watcher ran for the water and waded through. "We need to be on the other side of the water so we can cover them when they cross."

Swimming as fast as he could, Watcher made it across before the rest of the NPCs. The villagers quickly moved through the water and formed a firing line on the colorful island.

"Everyone, use your magic bows." Watcher took out the Fossil Bow of Destruction and drew back the string, flashing red as he took damage. "Shoot at the withers. We need to give Mirthrandos and her forces some help."

Aiming at the nearest wither, he released the string. A magical arrow streaked upward, sparkling as it pierced the air, then struck the monster. The magical shaft took all of the monster's HP just as the other NPCs released their arrows. The sky darkened with the enormous volley of arrows from the enchanted bows, the pointed shafts striking the withers in the back. Some of the monsters turned and fired at the villagers, but Planter was ready. She raised her shield just in time to block the flaming skulls.

"As soon as Planter lowers her shield, fire again." Watcher drew back on his bowstring again as pain surged through his body, the Bow of Destruction ravaging his health to power its enchantments.

Planter lowered the shield. Instantly, more arrows streaked into the air from the NPC group. The magical projectiles struck the airborne monsters, causing them to flash red with damage. Watcher's shot destroyed another wither, but his own health was getting dangerously low. Someone threw a potion of healing on him, the liquid quenching the pain surging through his body. He put away the Bow and drew the magical bow he'd taken from the Vault. Drawing back on the string, he took careful aim and released, then ducked behind Planter's shield again.

The withers had felt the sting of their arrows and were now moving back toward their position, firing as they flew. Planter's shield glowed bright as the magical flames surrounded the NPCs, keeping them safe.

The wolves and golems charged toward the mushroom island. As the first wolves splashed into the water, the withers turned their attack to the floundering animals.

"NO!" Planter screamed in defiance. She moved forward, extending her shield to encompass those struggling through the liquid. The NPCs fired again, raining pointed barbs onto the withers.

"My bows are all gone," an NPC said behind Watcher.

"So are mine," shouted another.

Watcher glanced over his shoulder. Piles of dust were forming around the feet of the NPCs as their enchanted bows disintegrated, their magic completely consumed.

Watcher kept firing as fast as he could, moving to Planter's side. As a wither launched a flaming skull at her, Watcher dropped the bow and drew Needle from his inventory. He batted the flaming skulls away, sending them back to their maker. The dark projectiles exploded in the face of the wither, causing it to take damage, then disappear, its HP consumed.

"Hurry, swim through the water." Watcher pulled a mechite out of the water just as another flaming skull headed toward them. Needle moved before Watcher could even think, knocking the deadly attack back toward another monster.

The golems now waded into the water, their height allowing them to keep their heads above water. They just walked through the ocean, their pace not changing a bit.

More arrows streaked up at the withers, but far fewer than before; the villagers were using their normal bows instead of the enchanted ones. Watcher fired his again, but it cracked, then shattered into dust. He reached out and dragged the last of the mechites out of the water, then pulled Planter back onto the mushroom island.

"Everyone move backward," Watcher said quietly. "Head for the portal."

The iron golems stayed at the front of the group, their legs fully extended as they tossed mechites and wolves at the withers. The metallic creatures landed with pinpoint accuracy, tearing into the dark monsters with their razor-sharp blades and teeth. Mirthrandos slid down the side of the golem she was riding and moved inside Planter's shield.

"I'm surprised to see you here," Watcher said. "I thought you'd decided to abandon us."

Mirthrandos glared at Watcher, then glanced down at the mechite at her side. Fixit stared up at Watcher, an expression of pride on his shiny face.

"Fixit here convinced me you were worth the trouble," the ancient wizard said. "If it weren't for him, I'd still be in Wizard City."

Watcher smiled down at the little mechanized creature and bowed his head. "Thank you," he said to the creature, then nodded to Mirthrandos.

A huge blast shook the ground; the withers were bombarding the golems. Flaming skulls were falling upon them, causing their steel skin to char and crack.

"We need to help them!" Watcher exclaimed.

Mirthrandos grabbed his arm and kept him from running out onto the battlefield. "We need to get to the portal," the wizard said. "The golems can take care of themselves, for now."

The NPCs continued to move backwards across the mushroom island, Planter's flaming shield surrounding them. Watcher glanced over his shoulder. He could see the portal, its sparkling green field lighting the iron ring around it with an emerald glow. A cluster of mooshrooms stood between them and the portal, the bright-red cows just milling about.

Suddenly, Krael screamed. "You won't escape me, boy!"

The wither king flew high into the air, then fired a

stream of flaming skulls at the space between the villagers and the portal. His attack fell upon the mooshrooms, enveloping the animals and the surface of the mushroom island in a blast of fire and ash. The bright-red creatures instantly disappeared, as did the terrain. The wither king kept firing, painting the landscape with his deadly attack. When the smoke cleared, a crater at least a dozen blocks deep surrounded the portal, making the magical doorway impossible to reach.

"What do we do now?" Blaster asked. "We'll never be able to reach the portal now."

Watcher stared at the portal, a burning rage filling his soul.

I'm tired of these withers trying to destroy everything, Watcher thought.

Then he saw one of the golems throw another mechite at a wither and had an idea.

"I know how we can get into the portal." Watcher glanced at Mirthrandos. "We'll need your help."

"Tell me what you need." The old woman smiled, a dangerous look in her ancient eyes.

Watcher quickly explained his plan to the wizard and the other villagers.

"But how will you keep the withers from attacking us while we do this?" Blaster asked. "This seems too dangerous."

They all ducked as a flaming skull sailed toward them, exploding on Planter's shield. The detonation made their ears ring.

"I have a way to keep them distracted." Watcher glanced at Mirthrandos. "Bring in the golems."

The wizard closed her eyes for a moment. Suddenly, the ground shook as the golems all retreated from the withers, bringing the wolves with their mechite riders with them. They all moved within Planter's bubble of purple flames.

"When I give the signal, start the plan," Watcher said.

"What will the signal be?" Blaster asked.

Watcher banged on the leg of a golem, making a ringing sound, then removed his diamond chest plate and put on his Elytra wings. The giant metal creature lowered a hand, allowing Watcher to climb in.

"Watcher, what are you doing?" Planter asked, a worried expression on her square face.

"I'm doing what needs to be done, for everyone."

"But you don't have to—"

He held up a hand, silencing her. "Wait, Planter. You were right, none of these magical items are more important than their wielders. People *are* more important than stuff, but right now, everyone I care about, all my friends here and in the Far Lands, are more important than me."

He sniffled as he choked back a tear. The thought of what would likely happen filled Watcher with a profound sadness. At that moment, everything seemed crystal clear: how he'd mistreated Planter; how stupid he'd been about being a wizard instead of just being Watcher . . . he realized how foolish he was. He'd probably never have a chance to make it right, but if all of them would be safe, then it was a fair trade.

"But what about you?" A tear trickled from her beautiful green eye.

"I am the wielder, not a weapon." Watcher put a hand on her shoulder. "But sometimes, things don't work out for the wielder . . . I'm guessing this is one of those times." Watcher turned toward Blaster, the Flail of Regret gripped firmly in his right hand. "This is the signal."

Blaster put a fist to his chest, giving Watcher a warrior's salute.

He glanced at Mirthrandos and nodded. She closed her eyes and relayed the instructions to the golem. The metal giant stood up straight with Watcher in its hand. Suddenly, the iron golem threw Watcher through the air like a spear, aiming for Krael. Watcher leaned forward, causing his wings to snap open.

"NOW . . . GO!" Watcher shouted to the NPCs as he flew through the air, heading straight for his enemy, the king of the withers.

CHAPTER 30

Krael just stared at Watcher as the boy-wizard flew toward him, surprised by the sight.

Watcher arced to the right at the last instant, moving toward the monster from the side; Krael glanced around, looking for his enemy, but he didn't know where to look. And then Watcher landed on the creature's shoulder.

Grabbing the nearest skull with his left hand, keeping himself from falling, Watcher pulled out the Flail of Regrets. He swung it with all his strength, smashing it down upon his enemy. The pointy spikes dug into the wither king's shadowy flesh. Krael screamed in pain and frustration. The wither turned his head and fired a flaming projectile. Watcher moved across Krael's shoulders, easily staying behind the terrifying skulls and avoiding the attack.

The other withers in the monster army, equally surprised, stopped their attack and just stared as their king and his adversary struggled in aerial combat. Watcher glanced at his friends and smiled; the golems were picking up NPCs and tossing them through the portal.

The villagers sailed across the mushroom island, some two at a time. As Blaster sailed through the air,

Watcher saw the boy glancing up at him over his shoulder, a concerned expression on his square face. Once all the NPCs were through, the golems started tossing the wolves and mechites, too. The animals howled with fear, then disappeared through the shimmering emerald field.

Watcher brought his attention back to his foe, smashing him again and again with his spiked weapon. Krael flashed red as he took damage, his HP dropping. The monster activated his sparkling shield, allowing him to regenerate his health. This caused the monster to slowly descend to the ground. Watcher kept up his attack, but the spiked ball bounced off the shield, doing little to no damage. The iron golems saw the wither descending closer to the ground and moved toward him, their legs extending to allow them to grab the wither king. Krael must have seen them waiting, for he dropped his shield and rose higher into the air.

Watcher glanced back at the portal. "I'm not gonna let you through that portal, Krael," he said.

"How are you gonna stop me?" the monster growled furiously.

The wither king moved closer to the portal, an angry wail coming from its left skull.

The golems surrounded the portal, some using their bodies to create steps for the other metal giants to climb up and pass through the sparkling green doorway.

Krael sent a trio of flaming skulls at the golems, the projectiles exploding against their shining skin. The blasts caused cracks to form across their metallic chests and arms, but the golems continued to climb through the portal.

"The Great War is over, Krael. What do you hope to accomplish?"

"Revenge," the monster hissed angrily. "My wife and my withers were imprisoned for no reason."

"You and your army were trying to destroy everyone and everything." Watcher wrapped his arm around the left skull, holding on tight, and brought the flail down again.

Krael grunted with pain. "You know nothing about it. I was created to fight my creators' battles, but then they turned on us, imprisoning everyone I cared for. You and the NPCs won't get the chance to do that again. I'll destroy all of you to protect my people." Krael suddenly grew silent as he floated up high into the air.

"It's not our fault the warlocks created and then betrayed you."

Krael laughed, as if he knew some great secret. "Warlocks . . . ha, you are truly a fool. It wasn't the monsters who created us; it was the wizards."

"What?!"

"Ha ha." Krael's left head chuckled an evil laugh. "They made us in response to the living weapons being created by the monster warlocks, but we had ideas of our own."

Watcher was stunned by this news. *Baltheron, how can this be?*

But the Flail remained silent.

"We can find peace if we work together. All this fighting solves nothing," Watcher said.

The wither was quiet, moving higher and higher into the air.

Getting a little nervous, Watcher shoved the Flail of Regrets into his inventory, then wrapped both arms tight around the left skull. As they passed through the cloud layer, Watcher glanced down at the distant ground; a fall from this height would be fatal, his Elytra wings likely useless; he'd be moving too quickly to open his wings without breaking them.

"Krael, there's always another way."

"You're right, boy," the wither king said. "There *is* another way . . . like this."

Suddenly, the left skull tilted its head back and bit into Watcher's wrist. Pain exploded through his arm, forcing him to let go of the monster's skull, and at the same time, Krael tilted backward quickly, causing Watcher to lose his balance. He swung his arms in the air, trying to regain his stability, but the wither tilted back even further. Finally, gravity won the contest of balance and Watcher fell, screaming in terror.

CHAPTER 31

Watcher plummeted through the air, tumbling completely out of control. He passed through the clouds like a meteor from the heavens, speeding up as he fell. He swung his arms about, trying to regain some control, but all it did was make him look like some kind of diamond-coated flightless bird. He knew if he opened his wings at this speed, they'd be torn to shreds.

Extending his arms and legs, he let them catch the wind and slow him down, but they did little at his incredible rate of descent. He needed something to catch the wind without tearing or breaking. Reaching into his inventory, he grabbed his shield and held it over his head, but the blast of the wind tore it from his grasp, sending the wooden rectangle tumbling away.

Reaching into his inventory again, he searched for something, anything, that might slow him down. And then his hands fell upon a ball of wrinkled cloth.

Of course! Tharus' cape.

Watcher pulled the cape out and held on to a corner with all his might. He spooled it out slowly, letting it catch the wind a little at a time. Then, grabbing the opposite corner with his other hand, he held the cape at arm's length, the brilliant cloth fluttering as it caught the wind.

He was slowing.

Soon he'd be able to open his wings, he hoped. The cape was slowing him down, but if he wasn't going slow enough, the Elytra would break, and he'd fall to his death.

"Have I decelerated enough yet?" Watcher waited for an answer, but all he heard was the blast of the wind and his heart beating like a drum. "I have to try . . . this better work."

Watcher leaned forward, allowing the wings to snap into place. Instantly, the wings bent and creaked under the strain, but the Mending enchantment his sister had put on them before she gave them to him was doing its job. Suddenly, instead of falling, he was flying. He stuffed the cape back into his inventory and smiled.

A roar of frustration filled the air.

"You won't escape me, wizard," Krael bellowed from above.

Instantly, Watcher banked to the left, then dove as a stream of flaming skulls shot past him, one of them grazing his left wing. He banked to the right and dove straight down, heading for the portal. The other withers were firing on the golems surrounding the portal, trying to destroy the last of the metal giants, but they held their ground. A wall of purple flames enveloped the portal, protecting them. Watcher could see Planter standing on the edge of the iron ring surrounding the shimmering emerald surface of the portal, her shield blazing with magical power. She stared up at him as he flew toward her, an expression of fear etched into her face as Watcher juked to the left and right, trying to make himself a difficult target to hit.

More flaming skulls streaked by, some close enough for the fire to singe his hair. A blast knocked him to the side and sent pain radiating throughout his body; one of the skulls had found its target. Gray swirls floated in front of his face, making it hard to see. He could no longer tell how much health he still had; it was the wither effect, caused by Krael's attack.

But it didn't matter; if he didn't make it through the portal, he'd have no chance for survival, regardless of how much HP he had right now.

Pulling his arms into his sides, Watcher leaned forward and traded altitude for speed. He was a blur, flying faster than he'd ever flown before. The portal was coming closer quickly. Planter's shield flickered as a huge barrage of flaming skulls exploded upon its iridescent surface. She grimaced, as if in pain, but held the shield up high, the magical shell protecting the golems who stood around the portal with their legs extended, their metallic bodies acting as another layer of protection for Planter and the portal.

Watcher tried to will himself to fly even faster as he shot through the air, flaming skulls following him on all sides. When he reached the shield generated by Planter's magic, Watcher tried to slow down, but it was too late; in a blink of an eye, he was at the portal.

Reaching out with an arm, Planter grabbed hold of Watcher, trying to help slow him down, but instead, she was pulled backward along with him, into the portal. They tumbled through the shimmering green field together and appeared in the Hall of Planes, crashing into the legs of an iron golem, both of them flashing red as they took damage.

But the collision had likely saved their lives. If they'd slid off the obsidian path, they would have both fallen into the emptiness of the Void, enclosing the Hall.

"Watcher, are you alright?" Blaster asked.

He helped his friend up as Cutter lifted Planter to her feet.

"Don't worry about me," Watcher said as he struggled for breath. "Destroy the portal."

Cutter pulled out one of the magical pickaxes and began smashing the iron blocks making up the portal.

Blaster took out a magical pickaxe as well and tore into the same cube. Sounds of battle came through the portal as the echoes of explosions filled the Hall of Planes like thunder.

"Mirthrandos, why aren't the other golems coming through the portal?" Watcher asked.

"That's not the plan," the wizard said. "Their job is to keep the withers out until we can close the portal."

"You mean they're sacrificing themselves for us?" Planter asked, a look of shocked horror on her face. "That's not right!"

"I agree," the old woman said. "But that's what's necessary."

Waves of heat flooded through the portal as the sound of more explosions came through the shimmering gateway. Then, suddenly, the detonations stopped.

"What happened?" Er-Lan asked.

"I don't know." Blaster stopped digging for a moment and moved closer to the emerald-green field. "Maybe we should peek through and see."

"That sounds like a terrible idea," Fencer said. She reached out and pulled Blaster away from the portal.

"I'm surprised to say it." Planter glanced at Fencer. "But I agree with her. We need to stay back."

Suddenly, Krael's terrifying heads came through the portal. The Crowns of Skulls atop his heads glowed dangerously bright, iridescent flames surrounding each. Shouting in rage, the monster fired a string of flaming skulls at the nearest golem. They smashed into it, shoving the creature off the narrow obsidian walkway that made up the Hall of Planes. The metal giant fell into the Void, disappearing from sight.

"Cutter, Blaster . . . hurry!" Watcher shouted.

Krael turned toward the voice and fired. Watcher dove to the ground, the skulls streaking over him, just barely grazing his back, then flying into the void.

"No more violence," Er-Lan said suddenly. "NO MORE VIOLENCE!"

The zombie's voice boomed through the Hall, amplified, just like Mirthrandos's had been. The sound shocked
everyone, especially Krael, who stopped his attack and
stared at the zombie. As Er-Lan grew more furious, a shimmering purple glow seeped out from beneath his armor,
covering his whole body. Krael's eyes grew wide with surprise as the glowing energy moved across the zombie's
body like a living organism, flowing around his legs and
chest and arms like some kind of lavender serpent.

Slowly, Er-Lan raised his arms toward the wither
king. With fists clenched, the zombie lunged toward
the dark creature, filling the Hall with thunder as he
screamed at the top of his voice. A ball of sparkling,
iridescent energy burst from the zombie's chest and
smashed into the wither, shoving the surprised monster
back through the portal and out of the Hall of Planes.

Er-Lan collapsed to the ground, and an instant
later, the iron block Blaster and Cutter were attacking
finally shattered, breaking the metallic ring. The shimmering green field within the ring flickered once, then
disappeared.

"Is the portal closed?" Fencer asked.

Watcher glanced at Mirthrandos; the old woman
nodded.

"We did it?" Planter asked.

"We did it!" Watcher exclaimed.

The NPCs broke their silence and shouted with joy.

"We stopped Krael and his army!" Cutter reached
out to give a high five to his neighbor, but found it was
Er-Lan, slowly climbing to his feet, a purple glow still
surrounding his body. The big warrior hesitated for
just an instant, then turned and gave the high five to
another NPC while he watched the glowing zombie out
of the corner of his eye.

Watcher moved to Er-Lan's side and embraced him,
both arms squeezing the zombie tight. "You saved the
day, Er-Lan. I don't know how it happened. Maybe some
of my magic leaked into you."

"Probably," Er-Lan replied, a guilty expression on his scarred face.

As Watcher released the hug and moved back, Er-Lan seemed to tense his own body, face creased in concentration. Slowly, the iridescent glow faded, seeping back through his chain mail armor, then disappearing. Er-Lan finally relaxed his body and gave Watcher a grin.

"Perhaps we should get out of the Hall of Planes," Mirthrandos said. "Though I don't know where you intend to go."

Watcher turned to the ancient wizard, then glanced at his companions.

"I think it's about time we headed back home."

"Home . . . where's that?" Mirthrandos asked. "My home is back there." She pointed at the dark and broken portal, shaking her head.

"Our village moved into the Wizard's Tower." Planter spoke with a sad expression on her face, as if she didn't look forward to going home.

"Ahh . . . the Wizard's Tower." The ancient wizard frowned. "That's where my punishment started."

"You mean that's where the wizards made you immortal?" Blaster asked.

The old woman nodded. "Not 'wizards,' but wizard; the big guy himself, Tharus, the most powerful of all the wizards."

"Well, that's where our home is now." Watcher put a hand on the ancient wizard's arm. "It can be your home as well."

"Well . . . we'll see. I don't have pleasant memories of that place." She flashed a smile at Watcher, then put an arm around Planter. "Let's get out of here. I think it's time the two women led this crazy band of warriors."

Planter smiled and took Mirthrandos's arm, then headed to the staircase that ascended into the darkness and out of the Hall of Planes.

CHAPTER 32

Watcher followed Mirthrandos and Planter up the dark stairway with Er-Lan at his side. The ancient wizard held her wooden staff over her head, then mumbled something. Bright purple flames enveloped the staff, making the metal-banded tip glow brighter than the sun, filling the passage with light and allowing everyone to see.

"Er-Lan, are you feeling okay after what happened back there?" Watcher asked.

The zombie shrugged. "Er-Lan does not know what Watcher means." He glanced over his shoulder, nervously, as if he were checking to see if others were listening.

"Well, sometimes when I use my magic it makes me feel tired." Watcher put a hand on the zombie's shoulder. "I figured if my magic somehow leaked into you and gave you those powers, you'd be tired as well."

"Ahh . . . yes . . . Er-Lan is tired from your magic."

The zombie glanced around again, as if he were trying to hide something.

"Are you alright?" Watcher asked. "You look so nervous."

"Er-Lan is fine!" he snapped. "There is nothing wrong with Er-Lan."

The zombie glared at Watcher, then turned and headed to the back of the company.

"Nice going," a voice said from behind.

Watcher turned and found Blaster smiling at him, Fencer at his side, as usual. The young boy sprinted up the steps to stand next to Watcher, the narrow passage not wide enough for Fencer to stay at his side.

"What was that all about?" Watcher asked.

Blaster shrugged. "Who knows? Maybe your magic left a bad taste in his mouth."

"Perhaps, but I wonder if—"

Suddenly, the entire stairway shook, as if something were hammering on the walls and floor.

"That's probably the iron golems," Blaster said.

"I figured they'd stay down there in the Hall of Planes with the Guardians." Watcher glanced over his shoulder.

The hulking metallic creatures were entering the stairway, each having to bend over to fit under the low ceiling. Their shining heads scraped the sandstone overhead, causing sand to fall, coating their heads with a fine layer of dust. The wolves barked at the golems, then ran between their legs, a mechite riding on each furry back. The mechanical animals sped up the stairs, streaming past the villagers and disappearing into the darkness up ahead.

Finally, they reached the end of the passage. Watcher was glad to step into the open air; the dusty passage made him feel as if dirt covered every inch of his body. The stairway had led them into a massive crater, scorch marks and ash covering the ground.

"What happened here?" Mirthrandos knelt and wiped her hand across the sooty blocks, then put her fingers to her nose and took in the burnt aroma.

"Krael destroyed the village here." Watcher climbed up to the top of the crater, then glanced down at his companions. "After the village was gone, he blasted this hole in the ground to find the entrance to the Hall of Planes."

The ancient wizard grew quiet as she glanced around at the destruction, her eyes tearing up as she stared at the charred remains of the village. "This was my village when I was a little girl. My parents grew up here and met beside the community well. Now, it's erased from the surface of Minecraft." Her sadness turned to anger, her body glowing bright with magical power. "Krael and the other withers have done such great harm to so many."

"Well, they won't be doing any more harm in this world." Blaster smiled. "We took care of that."

"Yeah, my Blaster destroyed that portal . . . he's a hero!" Fencer smiled at Blaster, then reached out to take his hand.

Blaster stared at the hand, then shook his head and moved away, a subtle, embarrassed grin creasing his square face.

Fencer sighed at first, but smiled when she saw the boy's grin.

"Krael destroyed so many lives in his quest for power and revenge," Mapper said. "He was truly a monster."

"That's how withers are," Mirthrandos said.

"Well, you'd know . . . right?" Watcher glared at Mirthrandos.

"What are you talking about?"

"Krael told me how the withers came into existence." Anger filled Watcher's voice.

The other NPCs gathered near and listened. He climbed to the edge of the crater and stared down at the ancient wizard, the iron golems gathering around her protectively.

"The wither king told me the wizards created him and the other withers to be used as a weapon in the Great War . . . is that true?"

Mirthrandos remained silent for a moment as all eyes shifted to her. Fixit moved next to her and stared up at the ancient wizard, an expression of shock and confusion on the tiny metal creature's face.

Reluctantly, the ancient wizard nodded.

Planter gasped, glancing at Watcher, then back to Mirthrandos. "They destroyed so many of our friends and neighbors, not to mention the destruction they're probably bringing to the creatures of the world we just left. How could you wizards be so stupid?"

"It was the idea of the strongest wizard, our leader, Tharus. He sometimes acted rashly, and didn't think things through." She sighed. "He did create the withers, as well as some other monsters, but his arrogance proved stronger than his common sense."

"What do you mean?" Mapper asked.

The old woman glanced around and found all eyes were on her, even the metallic eyes of her companions from Wizard City. "Tharus made the withers as strong and violent and smart as possible, so they could destroy the monsters and their living weapons, like the Broken Eight. But he thought he'd be able to control them, as long as he and two other wizards controlled all the Crowns of Skulls. He never imagined the withers would take one. I think you met the one that tricked him and stole the first Crown?"

"Kaza," Blaster hissed.

Mirthrandos nodded. "After he stole the first Crown, it was clear the wizards couldn't control the withers. Kaza and the other withers switched sides and fought for the monster warlocks. That was when Tharus hid the second crown, and the third was used as bait to get those monsters into the Cave of Slumber."

"It seems you wizards caused your own undoing," Blaster said. "Perhaps wizards aren't so trustworthy, after all."

Planter nodded, then glanced at Watcher. She gave him an *I told you so* look.

"Well, all that's in the past now." Watcher smiled at Planter, but she looked away. He sighed. "I think it's time we head home; we have a long walk ahead of us."

"At least there isn't an army of monsters chasing us this time." Blaster smiled. "That's a nice change."

"I'll second that." Mapper laughed, causing other NPCs to chuckle. He pulled out his map, then glanced at the clouds overhead to see which direction was west; the sun directly overhead was no help. "This way." The old man pointed to the distant horizon and started walking, the rest of their party following close behind.

Watcher moved next to Planter. They walked in silence for a while, the tension building. One of the mechanical wolves moved next to Planter with Fixit riding on the creature's back. The silver-haired mechite seemed to like Planter and had stayed at her side since escaping into the Hall of Planes.

"Planter, I don't want there to be any secrets between us." Watcher looked at her, but she kept her eyes on the ground. "I know you hate all this magic, but it was necessary to stop Krael and his wither army."

He paused for a moment to let her speak. She remained silent. "If you hadn't used your powers and your shield, we'd likely be dead, and the withers would be destroying the Far Lands right now. You saved a lot of lives."

Her silence just added to the tension between the two of them.

Watcher sighed. "I just want things to go back to the way they were . . . you know, you and me . . . boyfriend and girlfriend."

She slowly raised her head and glanced at him. A tear was trickling down her cheek, her beautiful green eyes red and bloodshot from sadness. "I'm not me anymore."

She pointed to her glowing arms and the magical armor wrapped around her body. "All this magic has changed me in ways I don't understand. Part of who I am has been sucked into that magical shield. Every time I touch it, I lose a little more of myself. I can feel it right now, tugging at the back of my mind, drawing memories from me and replacing them with thoughts I don't even understand."

"Then we should get rid of the shield."

"No!" Planter moved away from him, a look of terror in her eyes. She glanced around; everyone was staring at her in shock. "That'll be worse. I don't understand it, but I know I have to keep that shield with me at all times, or something terrible will happen." Planter sighed. "It's a part of me, forever, all because of magic. Until I figure this out, and I get this shield thing out of my mind, there is no you and me, no boyfriend and girl-friend. There's just Watcher and Planter, separate, but friends . . . sort of. Can you handle that?"

"Well, since I don't have much of a choice, I can han-dle that." Watcher smiled at her, trying to ease her wor-ries. "But I can't guarantee I won't watch out for you all the time."

"I'm okay with that." She relaxed a little, then smiled. "I'm just looking forward to life going back to normal again."

"Me too," Watcher replied. "Race you to the top of that sand dune? That is, if you think you're still faster than me."

"I always have been, and I still am." She laughed, then took off running, Watcher a step behind.

Planter's laughter seemed to infect the rest of the party, the villagers all laughed as well as they sprinted for the distant dune. Even the golems ran, shining smiles on their metallic faces. The ground shook with their gigantic steps, but no one was afraid. For the first time in a long time, their company was happy and could run just for the feel of the wind streaming through their hair.

Watcher reached the top of the sand dune a step behind Planter, her laughter and the laughter from the other NPCs music to his soul.

And for the first time in a long time, he felt safe and happy.

AVAILABLE NOW FROM MARK CHEVERTON AND SKY PONY PRESS

  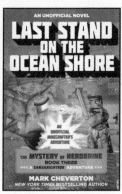

THE MYSTERY OF HEROBRINE SERIES
Gameknight999 must save his friends from an evil virus intent on destroying all of Minecraft!

Gameknight999 was sucked into the world of Minecraft when one of his father's inventions went haywire. Trapped inside the game, the former griefer learned the error of his ways, transforming into a heroic warrior and defeating powerful Endermen, ghasts, and dragons to save the world of Minecraft and his NPC friends who live in it.

Gameknight swore he'd never go inside Minecraft again. But that was before Herobrine, a malicious virus infecting the very fabric of the game, threatened to destroy the entire Overworld and escape into the real world. To outsmart an enemy much more powerful than any he's ever faced, the User-that-is-not-a-user will need to go back into the game, where real danger lies around every corner. From zombie villages and jungle temples to a secret hidden at the bottom of a deep ocean, the action-packed adventures of Gameknight999 and his friends (and, now, family) continue in this thrilling follow-up series for Minecraft fans of all ages.

Trouble in Zombie-town (Book One):
$9.99 paperback • 978-1-63450-094-4

The Jungle Temple Oracle (Book Two):
$9.99 paperback • 978-1-63450-096-8

Last Stand on the Ocean Shore (Book Three):
$9.99 paperback • 978-1-63450-098-2

AVAILABLE NOW FROM MARK CHEVERTON AND SKY PONY PRESS

HEROBRINE REBORN SERIES
Gameknight999 and his friends and family face Herobrine in the biggest showdown the Overworld has ever seen!

Gameknight999, a former Minecraft griefer, got a big dose of virtual reality when his father's invention teleported him into the game. Living out a dangerous adventure inside a digital world, he discovered that the Minecraft villagers were alive and needed his help to defeat the infamous virus, Herobrine, a diabolical enemy determined to escape into the real world.

Gameknight thought Herobrine had finally been stopped once and for all. But the virus proves to be even craftier than anyone could imagine, and his XP begins inhabiting new bodies in an effort to escape. The User-that-is-not-a-user will need the help of not only his Minecraft friends, but his own father, Monkeypants271, as well, if he has any hope of destroying the evil Herobrine once and for all.

Saving Crafter (Book One):
$9.99 paperback • 978-1-5107-0014-7

Destruction of the Overworld (Book Two):
$9.99 paperback • 978-1-5107-0015-4

Gameknight999 vs. Herobrine (Book Three):
$9.99 paperback • 978-1-5107-0010-9

AVAILABLE NOW FROM MARK CHEVERTON AND SKY PONY PRESS

THE BIRTH OF HEROBRINE SERIES
Can Gameknight999 survive a journey one hundred years into Minecraft's past?

A freak thunderstorm strikes just as Gameknight999 is activating his father's Digitizer to reenter Minecraft. Sparks flash across his vision as he is sucked into the game . . . and when the smoke clears he's arrived safely. But it doesn't take long to realize that things in the Overworld are very different.

The User-that-is-not-a-user realizes he's been accidentally sent a hundred years into the past, back to the time of the historic Great Zombie Invasion. None of his friends have even been born yet. But that might be the least of Gameknight999's worries, because traveling back in time also means that the evil virus Herobrine, the scourge of Minecraft, is still alive . . .

The Great Zombie Invasion (Book One):
$9.99 paperback • 978-1-5107-0994-2

Attack of the Shadow-crafters (Book Two):
$9.99 paperback • 978-1-5107-0995-9

Herobrine's War (Book Three):
$9.99 paperback • 978-1-5107-0996-7

AVAILABLE NOW FROM MARK CHEVERTON AND SKY PONY PRESS

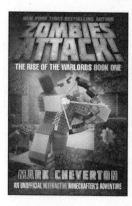  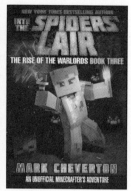

THE RISE OF THE WARLORDS SERIES
A brand-new Minecraft fiction series from Mark Cheverton explores the mysterious borders of the Overworld!

The Far Lands is a hidden, mystical area located at the very edge of Minecraft's outer borders, unknown to normal users. There, the life of a young boy named Watcher is suddenly turned upside down when his village is destroyed by a vile warlord.

That single event sets off a chain of unexpected events, as Watcher and a handful of his friends vow to save their friends and bring the warlords responsible to justice. But along the way, they'll uncover a terrifying secret about the monsters in the Far Lands, one that could change Minecraft forever.

EXCERPT FROM
THE WITHER INVASION
A BRAND-NEW FAR LANDS ADVENTURE

The NPCs moved quietly through the forest while the sun descended toward the western horizon. Few spoke; their fear of the monsters that were likely hunting them created a strained tension, stretching their courage almost to its breaking point. The iron creatures from Mira's world formed a protective ring around the company, giving the villagers a faint sense of safety, but it was barely an echo compared to the thunderstorm of dread rumbling through their minds.

After they'd been running for a couple of hours, the forest biome morphed into a frozen river. The air changed from a pleasant breeze filled with the smell of leaves and grass and flowers to one with a frigid bite; tiny ice crystals riding the wind dug into exposed skin. With the flat landscape, there was no protection from the icy gusts, causing the NPCs to cluster together for warmth.

"I've never enjoyed these frozen biomes," Blaster complained as he removed his dark green armor and replaced it with white. "All these areas offer is a lot of snow and ice."

"And don't forget polar bears," Mapper added. "Like the one we came across when we were looking for the witches."

"I remember." Planter nodded as she walked up a small mound of snow, her feet making a crunching sound.

"My mom saw that bear too . . . right?" Fencer's voice quivered. "She was . . . still . . . alive?"

Planter nodded. "Yes, Saddler saw the bear. She thought it was beautiful." She held her shield up for Fencer to see. "We found a shield like mine just before we saw the polar bear. It was given to your mom, to keep her safe."

"It didn't work very well, did it?" Fencer sniffled as a tear tumbled down her cheek. She moved to Planter's side, her feet slipping on some ice. She reached out and grabbed Planter's shoulder for support. "What happened to the shield?"

Planter glanced at Watcher, then to Cutter and Blaster; they all shrugged. "I'm not sure. After she was . . . well . . . after the spider . . ."

"You're trying to say, 'after she was killed?'" Fencer asked, looking straight into Planter's eyes.

The young wizard nodded, her emerald eyes tearing up. "Yeah. After she was killed, it was pretty crazy. I'm not sure what happened to her shield."

"Too bad," Fencer sniffled again. "I'd like to have it; maybe it would remind me of my mom."

"Er-Lan knows where it is." The zombie scurried across a frozen river, his clawed feet digging into the ice, making a sharp scraping sound. He moved to Fencer's side and reached into his inventory, pulling out the enchanted shield as well as a decorated pickaxe. "Er-Lan picked it up after the battle, as well as Saddler's pickaxe, and forgot they were here. This zombie doesn't understand the significance of the pickaxe, but it was—"

"You have my dad's pick?" Fencer reached out and took the iron tool from Er-Lan's hand. She hugged it as if it were a long-lost sibling.

"Er-Lan did not know these were important. It was just—"

"You were hiding these things all this time?" Cutter glared suspiciously at the zombie. "Why did you keep them a secret? What other secrets do you have?"

Er-Lan glanced at Cutter, eyes wide, then turned to Fencer and handed her the shield. Still in tears, the young girl took the shield with her left hand, and it brushed against the identical shield held by Planter. Instantly, a bright flash of purple light filled the air, knocking Planter to her knees with a blast of magical power. Er-Lan moved to help his friend, but Cutter grabbed the zombie by the back of his chain mail and pulled him away.

"You aren't touching her." Cutter glared at him. "Keep your slimy green hands to yourself.

The big NPC stood between the zombie and the girls, his hand reaching for his weapon.

"Now calm down, Cutter. Er-Lan is a friend, and you know that." Mapper put a hand on the big warrior's arm, pulling it to his side. "We're grateful the shield and pick-axe were saved. They're obviously important to Fencer."

Cutter glanced at the young girl. Fencer was hugging both the shield and pickaxe while Planter climbed to her feet.

Er-Lan stared up at Cutter, then lowered his gaze and shuffled away, his clawed feet crunching through the snow.

"I still think there's something going on with that zombie." Cutter glared at Er-Lan, then brought his gaze to Watcher. "I don't trust him, and neither should you."

Watcher sighed. The conflict between Cutter and Er-Lan made everyone feel more stressed. "Cutter, I would trust my life to Er-Lan. He's saved me countless times, and I have no reason to doubt his dedication."

"Well, he's never saved me, and I bet he never will." The hulking warrior turned from the young wizard and trudged away through the snow, an angry scowl etched into his square face.

"I doubt he will if you keep accusing Er-Lan of being a traitor," Blaster said behind him.

"What?!" Cutter boomed over his shoulder.

"Nothing . . . nothing." Blaster stepped away from the warrior, hoping to avoid becoming the target of his anger.

"That's enough arguing," Watcher shouted. "All this tension is gonna tear us apart."

He slowed to a walk and turned to glanced at the rest of their company. They had maybe seventy NPCs in their little army, many of them elderly or very young. Fear was evident in all of their eyes; they knew the wither king was still out there, hunting them, and the internal strife wasn't helping.

"We need to help each other and not resort to blaming or accusing. The only way we'll survive this conflict with the withers is to work together." He glanced at Cutter. "All of us are in this together. There are no traitors here, just friends and family, and that's what makes us stronger than the monsters."

"You think family is gonna help us defeat Krael and his army?" Cutter asked.

"No," Watcher said. The other NPCs were shocked.

"It isn't family that will let us defeat them, it's the fact that we'll do anything to help each other." He turned from Cutter and cast his gaze across the villagers. "Together, we are stronger than the monsters. But we must remember what's important . . . which is that no one is alone." He paused to let it sink in for a moment. "Everyone has an army at their back, ready to protect them. If we work together and watch each other's backs, then the withers will fail. Remember, if we—"

A wolf howled suddenly, the sound cutting through the icy landscape.

"Monsters coming." Er-Lan's voice sounded scared. "A lot of them."

"You hear that in the howl?" Blaster asked.

Er-Lan nodded.

"Up ahead, I see some extreme hills," Mapper said, pointing with a wrinkled finger. "Maybe we can lose them in the valleys."

"Right." Watcher nodded. "Anyone too weak to run, the golems will carry you."

He glanced at Mirthrandos. The ancient wizard closed her eyes for a moment as she relayed the commands to the metal giants, then opened them and nodded. The iron and obsidian golems reached down and picked up the grandparents and grandchildren in the party.

"Come on!" Watcher turned and sprinted for the snow-covered hills up ahead. A wave of silver streaked past him as the iron wolves and their mechite riders raced ahead to make sure it would be safe.

Glancing over his shoulder, Watcher looked for their pursuers. In the distance, he could see dark shapes moving across the frozen landscape; the monsters were clumped together in a large group, making it difficult to tell their number, but however many there were, he was sure it would be too many.

The NPCs ran as fast as they could, their feet kicking snow up into the air. Many stumbled and fell as they crossed the frozen river that wound its way across the landscape. Other villagers reached down and helped the fallen to their feet, then kept going, fear keeping their legs pumping.

When they reached the extreme hills biome, Watcher charged into a narrow valley, steep hills lining the sides.

"You sure . . . being in a narrow valley is . . . a good idea?" Mapper asked, struggling to catch his breath.

"It'll make a larger force easier to confront." Watcher offered the old man a bottle of water. "Confined in these valleys, the monsters won't be able to use their overwhelming numbers to surround us."

"But it could make escape for us more difficult, right?" Mapper sounded worried.

"Don't worry, these valleys always have an exit." Watcher smiled at the old man, hoping to appear confident, though it was a lie; he was terrified.

As they ran between the steep hills, Watcher noticed many snow-covered outcroppings extending over the passes. Structures of stone and gravel stretched out from these peaks, at times even spreading out high overhead across the narrow passes.

Suddenly, a group of wolves howled and returned, barking and growling to the mechites and Mirthrandos. Skidding to a stop, Watcher glanced at Er-Lan, unsure what was wrong.

"The wolves say it is a dead end up ahead," the zombie said. "There is no exit that way."

"Then we need to go back." Watcher turned around, but was greeted by more growls from the other end of the narrow pass. He glanced at the zombie.

"The monsters have entered the pass." Er-Lan moved to Watcher and placed a hand on his shoulder. "Many are there, blocking the exit."

Growls and snarls floated through the cold air as the monsters slowly moved through the cliff-lined pass toward the villagers.

"So . . . we're trapped?" Watcher glanced at the zombie, hoping for a different answer than he knew he'd get.

Er-Lan lowered his eyes to the ground, then nodded. "The wolves report there are many monsters approaching."

"How many?"

The zombie took a nervous swallow, then spoke in a hushed voice. "Far too many . . . we're trapped, with no hope of escape."

Glancing up at the steep hills, Watcher looked for some way out. The hills were made of stone and gravel, with a few blocks of coal-ore here and there. Every flat surface was covered with snow as soft flakes drifted down from the cloudy sky overhead. The sides of the hills were steep, at some places completely sheer. They'd never be able to climb their way out.

"What's the plan?" someone asked, but Watcher didn't really hear; he was completely overwhelmed with grief. He'd led them into a hopeless position, from which it seemed escape was impossible.

"What do we do?"

"Watcher . . . use your magic."

"Watcher . . . save us."

Every terrified voice drove another icicle of guilt into the young wizard's soul.

I was trying to save these people, and now I've doomed them. Fear and panic filled Watcher's mind, making it difficult to think.

The snarling voices of the monsters were getting louder . . . they were coming.

Someone shouted out for the NPCs to build defenses, but Watcher knew they would do no good; by the sound of the horde, he could tell these were the warped monsters Krael had brought with him from the distorted lands. They were stronger than regular monsters and could do things others couldn't.

"Here they come!" Cutter shouted. "Everyone get to the barricade."

Walls wouldn't stop the monsters, nor would arrows or swords . . . there just weren't enough NPCs here to stop this mob. It was hopeless, and it was all Watcher's fault. He wanted to just give up and disappear, but he knew he didn't have long to wait—death was coming for them all.

This was the end.

COMING SOON:

THE WITHER INVASION: WITHER WAR BOOK THREE